Also by Brianna DuMont:

Famous Phonies: Legends, Fakes and Frauds Who Changed History

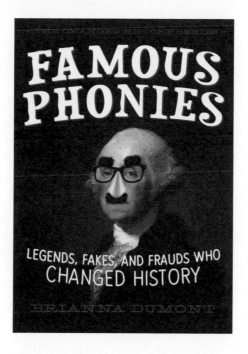

*Fantastic Fugitives: Criminals, Cutthroats, and Rebels
Who Changed History (While on the Run!)*

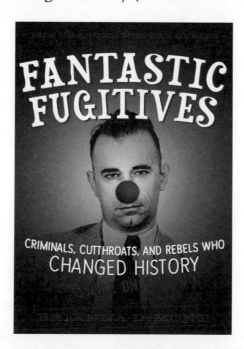

THRILLING THIEVES

THE CHANGED HISTORY SERIES

THRILLING THIEVES

LIARS, CHEATS, AND CONS WHO CHANGED HISTORY

BRIANNA DuMONT

Sky Pony Press

NEW YORK

Visit our website at www.skyponypress.com.
www.briannadumont.com

10 9 8 7 6 5 4 3 2 1

Library of Congress Cataloging-in-Publication Data available on file.

Hardcover ISBN: 978-1-5107-0169-4
Paperback ISBN: 978-1-5107-5138-5
Ebook ISBN: 978-1-5107-5140-8

Cover photo: WikiCommons
Cover design by Georgia Morrissey
Interior illustrations by Bethany Straker
Interior design by Joshua Barnaby

Printed in China

Contents

Author's Note

I hope you have as much fun reading this book as I had writing it. To me, villains are exciting to research, because they tend not to bind themselves to morality codes as rigorously as the "good guys." Which brings me to another point: even here, they're not all bad. Some of the thieves are actually the good guys in disguise. (And some just think they're the good guys in disguise.) But for the truly dreadful acts, is it fair to judge them by our modern lens? Or are some things evil no matter what or where? By whose standards of morality should these line-crossers be judged?

Think about this as you read the tales of Elizabeth I, Francisco Pizarro, and Madame Cheng, and remember: it's never just the "facts" in history. Interpretations of the same event can and *will* change over time. So, have fun—and if any thief catches your interest, I've listed my sources and my personal notes on sources for you to draw your own conclusions. If you're doing a report, my citations and tons of extra information on these thieves can be downloaded on my website: www.briannadumont.com.

"Everybody steals. . . . I've stolen a lot, myself. But I know how to steal!"
—Thomas Edison, *Harper's* Magazine, 1932

enter at your own risk

Introduction

Caution: Don't Look for the Good Guys in Here

What do Honest Abe, Mother Theresa, and Gandhi have in common? They're all too good for this book, that's what! In here, you'll find miscreants, rogues, and all sorts of line-crossers. Of course, a book on stealing wouldn't be complete without a spy or two, so keep your eyes peeled.

Some faces may seem angelic (and famous), but don't be fooled. Every single person you'll read about here has stolen their way into history, changing it forever.

It's not only the obvious ones, like the *Mona Lisa*–pocketing Vincenzo Peruggia or Pirate Queen Madame Cheng. They're clearly criminals. It's the other ones that might take you by surprise, like Robert Fortune, a simple gardener from Scotland who stole China's greatest secret—how to grow tea. Or the father of the lightbulb, Thomas Edison, who stole everything but his name. (Yes, seriously.)

If you think villains have too long been overlooked, or you just really want to see the bad guys win for once, you're in luck. Turn the page and follow these twelve troublemakers as they construct the Louvre museum in Paris, modernize New York City, and even create Hollywood—all through their thieving ways.

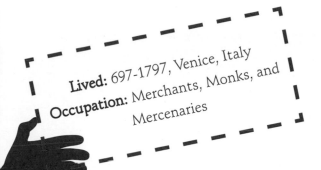

Lived: 697–1797, Venice, Italy

Occupation: Merchants, Monks, and Mercenaries

Venice

Not Just a Pretty Face

Today, Venice is a tourist hot spot known for her beauty and history. For the medieval Venetians, however, life wasn't all masquerade parties and gondola rides. They were powerful, business-minded people who went weak in the knees at the sight of silk, salt, and stacks of cash. At one time, Venice controlled the Mediterranean shipping lanes. From Egyptian pepper to Russian furs and beeswax, Venice could get anybody what they wanted, and that made the city powerful.

The Venetians knew they were awesome and wanted everyone else to accept it, too. They called their city the Most Serene Republic of Venice (*La Serenissima*, for short) and waited to be worshipped. From the thirteenth to the fifteenth century, they were. The question is, how did a tiny, floating city in northern Italy get so powerful?

They stole it all, of course.

*Life wasn't all about gondola rides down the Grand Canal for the Venetians.
It was also about money.*

Monkish Mayhem

It all started in 828 CE when someone stole a corpse. At the time, the pope in Rome didn't want Christians trading with Muslims. It might make the Christians think new thoughts, and everyone knew how dangerous thinking was. That didn't sound like good business sense to the Venetians, especially when there were Muslims across the world who had access to exotic spices like pepper. Before refrigeration, spoiled meat tasted much better with pepper.

Not having any land where they could grow food themselves, the Venetians had to be smart—they had to trade for what they needed. Despite promising the pope that they'd stay away from Muslims, two Venetian merchants named Buono and Rustico traveled to Alexandria, Egypt—a Muslim-controlled city—where they met two Greek monks who were getting tired of living there.

Together, the four hatched a plan to steal the eight-hundred-year-old body of St. Mark from his church and smuggle it aboard the Venetians' ship. In the

Middle Ages, everyone knew that a saint's body could only be moved if the saint allowed it. If St. Mark would rather stay put, he'd get impossibly heavy or take some other drastic action to show his displeasure. If the saint allowed himself to be moved, it was actually considered a rescue!

The four thieves tiptoed into the tomb, pried off the stone lid, and slashed the back of the silk cloth in which the body was wrapped. Extremely carefully, they pulled out the corpse and replaced it with another one. By only cutting the back of the silk wrapping, the thieves left all the security seals attached to the front in place. If anyone came looking, everything would look normal from the top, which was lucky, because dead saints have one other trick under their halos: they have a powerful smell. Don't worry, it's not eau de rotting corpse; it's sweet!

The pleasant odor acted like an alarm system. Before the four thieves could sneak out of the church, the Alexandrian priests knew something was up because of the smell. They went to check the seals, but since everything looked intact, they shrugged and went back to praying.

Just a spritz.

There was only one more obstacle for the thieves: the Muslim port inspectors. Buono and Rustico had a plan for that, too. Islamic law forbids the eating of pork. In fact, these medieval Muslims didn't even want to touch the stuff! So the Venetians hid the body at the bottom of a barrel and stuffed a bunch of raw pork cutlets on top. The Muslim inspectors quickly passed the barrels through.

Safely on their ship, the thieves relaxed and fell asleep while the body pickled under pork. That is, until a storm drove the ship dangerously close to some rocks. No one woke up. Well, no one except for St. Mark. According to his biographer (centuries later), St. Mark somehow alerted the sailors just in time to steer them away from disaster. Soon, the ship with its precious cargo sailed safely into the Venetian harbor.

Whew! That stinks worse than your feet!

doge:

Like a governor, a doge was the senior elected official in Venice. Unlike a governor, the doge had to be a man, and old (no set rules, but gray hair was best). He held the position for life, but could be kicked out of office and exiled by the people of Venice.

The merchants weren't even given a slap on the wrist when they got back to Venice. Instead, they got a big parade where the **doge** praised their cunning. The doge even had the body placed in his own private palace and ordered a church built for it.

The Venetians wallpapered their city with references to St. Mark and his lion symbol. Their entire identity as a city now centered on the Egyptian saint. Every new success, business venture, and military victory was thanks to St. Mark. The Venetians thought they were winning *because* of St. Mark. (Modern historians read it as Venice giving itself the go-ahead to do whatever it wanted.)

This included declaring themselves independent from Rome. The Venetians insisted that **St. Mark** had practically begged the Venetians to take him. Those bones were a powerful ace up their silk sleeves, and they took full advantage by ignoring Roman authority and trading with anyone and everyone—even the off-limits Muslims.

The pope didn't like the Venetians because they always put business first, but Venice didn't care. She luxuriated in her fancy goods and sold rare, purple Syrian silks to the rest of Italy. This didn't make Venice a world power yet, but her next theft would.

Now that they'd stolen and adopted a relic for themselves without any lightning bolts, vengeful earthquakes, or sinking cities, nothing would stop the Venetians from doing it again, and again, and again.

The World's Longest Detour

With the arrival of a person as important as St. Mark, the Venetians needed somewhere lavish to keep him, so they built a brand-new basilica (church) and gave it a really creative name: St. Mark's Basilica. When it burned down in the tenth century,

St. Mark:

The Venetians accidently lost St. Mark's body for a while in the tenth century after a fire, but he miraculously popped up in the eleventh century. That's the story according to legend, anyway. Hey, when's the last time anyone saw Giovanni?

Monks Who Steal Stuff

Medieval monks are known for being pious and praying a lot. While that's true, some medieval monks had more than their religion on their minds. A number of them were only thinking about pride and profit. Before two Greek monks helped steal St. Mark's body for the pride (and profit) of Venice, two other Greek monks did the same for Byzantine emperor Justinian in 552 CE.

China had the best silk around, and emperors like having the best. What emperors don't like is paying a lot for the best. History doesn't know exactly what Justinian offered, but he talked two monks into venturing eastward to discover the secret of Chinese silk production. The monks traveled to China, stole silk-spitting worms, hid them in bamboo canes, and made off into the night. Not only did their theft smash China's monopoly on silk, but it turned the Persians' Silk Road into more of a spice road. The trade in precious silk became one of the biggest money makers for Byzantine emperors. But, as we all know, what goes around comes around.

they built a new one for him, even nicer than the last. Now, they wanted to fill it up with more golden goodies.

Luckily for the Venetians, Europe was crusader-crazy. And where there were crusades, there was loot.

Once the pope called for the Fourth Crusade to take Jerusalem from the Muslims, the 35,000 crusaders from all over Europe asked the Venetians to build their boats. Instead of marching, the three Frenchmen in charge decided it would be nicer to sail. They ordered everyone to meet up in Venice. The crusaders needed so many boats they couldn't afford to pay Venice upfront for all of them.

Sensing a good deal, the Venetians agreed to build them anyway and even join the crusade—in exchange for something they wanted. They asked the crusaders to attack a Christian city south of Venice called **Zara** before heading to Jerusalem. The crusaders could spend the coming winter in the rich city of Zara—and they could loot it, too. Feeling kind of icky about it (and even though the pope forbade anybody from touching Zara), the crusaders still agreed and claimed the city after less than two weeks of siege.

Zara:

The city of Zara had once been under Venetian supervision, but they'd rebelled. Venice didn't appreciate it when good trading cities left them, and desperately wanted Zara's business back. Three previous attacks by the Venetians had all failed.

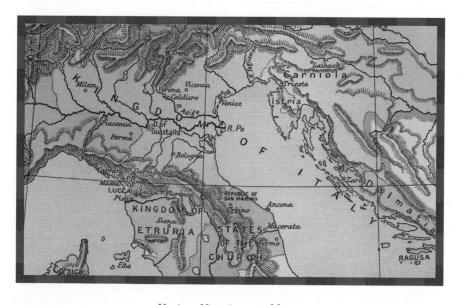

Venice: Not nice neighbors.

While the crusaders spent the winter in comfortable Zara, a claimant to the throne of **Constantinople** showed up and asked the crusaders for help getting rid of his ruling uncle.

Obviously, Constantinople doesn't have a ton to do with conquering Jerusalem. But the claimant, Alexius Angelus, promised to help the crusaders with their debt and even join the crusade himself if they helped him take over Constantinople. Another dubious detour was in the works.

> **Constantinople:**
> A Byzantine city in modern-day Turkey (today called Istanbul).

Despite the fact that Constantinople was the largest city any of the crusaders had seen, and that the city's walls had never been breached, the crusaders (including the Venetians) thought it was a great idea to try to invade it. As the crusaders sailed into battle, the blind, ninety-six-year-old Venetian doge stood in full armor urging everyone forward while arrows flew past his head. Physically, he never moved from the front of the boat, but he still inspired and shamed the crusading knights into attacking the walls. Constantinople's resident emperor fled the next day. The crusaders were let in, and so was Alexius.

Everything seemed great, except that new Emperor Alexius IV couldn't come up with the money owed to the Venetians, either. The Byzantine people got so tired of the young emperor trying

Zara: This feels weird . . .

Imagine scaling this while rocks and arrows streak past your ears.

to squeeze more money out of them that it wasn't long before someone squeezed *him*.

With the emperor dead, there was only one thing left to do. The Venetians decided to pay themselves. It was thieving time again.

Auditioning to Be the World's Next Great Empire

Venice had an "It's Complicated" sort of relationship with Constantinople. From the sixth century CE, the Byzantine emperors and Venice worked well together. Constantinople promised free trading privileges in exchange for Venetian support.

It was a sticky web that kept Venice closely connected to Constantinople. They didn't agree to this whole crusade caper with the *intention* of destroying their trading partner—that would have threatened all their business in the region. But one thing led to another, which led to another . . . and suddenly cities were being sacked.

For three days in April 1204, the Venetian crusaders and their European counterparts took anything of value they could find in Constantinople (including stuff that was nailed down, like huge, silver-plated altars). From palaces to the shop down the street, no one and nowhere was safe. Crusaders were supposed to leave churches alone and focus on the non-Christian sections of the city, such as the Muslim and Jewish quarters. They were also supposed to pool whatever they got to equally distribute the loot, but none of that happened. Countless objects made of precious metals, candlesticks, ancient art, and coins were melted down for the crusaders' personal greed.

Pretty soon, the whole city of Constantinople was stripped of all the jewels and precious metals the crusaders could stuff under their armor. Opportunistic crusaders brought their pack mules into churches in order to drag away more treasures, and they didn't care where the animals did their business. Constantinople, one of the great cities of the world, was turned into a gigantic river of feces and blood and melted metal. Anyone who tried to stop the thieving ended up dead. Finally, the rest of the crusaders had scavenged enough to pay the Venetians, who had already made out like bandits with their own looting.

Dating from 300 CE, the four tetrarchs used to be in Constantinople, but today hang out in St. Mark's Basilica in Venice, thanks to the Venetians' looting.

But the Venetians' doge ended up being the greatest thief of them all. Despite being blind, if he thought something was pretty, he shipped it straight back to Venice. On the plus side, that at least kept

Hippodrome:

A track for chariot racing dating from Roman times. Hippo means horse in ancient Greek and drome means path (although the Hippodrome of Constantinople is really a Roman circus—meaning it held public events other than horse racing).

some of the ancient art from the melting pot, including the four bronze horses from the famous **Hippodrome**. The horses, along with St. Mark, became the eternal symbol of Venice, where they still reside today.

The Venetians sent back treasures and relics, including drops of milk from the Virgin Mary, blood from Jesus, five more saints, jewels, marble columns, and a splinter from the Cross. They claimed the old Byzantine Empire as their own and shipped it off, relic by relic, to keep St. Mark's body company back home.

By keeping the stolen loot in their own city, Venetians were broadcasting a clear message to the rest of the world: we are a rising power. They were the new empire on the block, and thanks to their thieving ways, they had the goods to prove it.

If Napoleon Comes Calling

Napoleon was like a human metal detector, always sniffing out the best stuff to ship back to France during his many wars of conquest in the eighteenth and nineteenth century. When he defeated Venice in 1797, he looted the four bronze horses the Venetians had stolen from Constantinople. They got an even grander parade through the city of Paris on their way to their new home in the Louvre (see chapter 5). Since they symbolized Venice, Napoleon's theft broadcast to the world that his empire was the new top power.

With Napoleon's grand defeat in 1815, a Venetian sculptor lassoed the four horses back to Venice where crowds met them with an equally grand ceremony, including a twenty-one-gun salute. Although today the originals are kept inside St. Mark's Basilica for protection from the elements (and handsy tourists), replicas hang outside the basilica, exactly as they were after the Fourth Crusade.

A Brave New Marble World

The Fourth Crusade never made it past Constantinople, but it changed history all the same. With all their new stuff, the Venetians began building the city tourists know and love today. Their wood houses and dirt streets became marble masterpieces, and they filled their piazzas, palazzos, markets, and basilicas with stolen Byzantine

*The four horses are Venice's most iconic symbols
and date to approximately 400 CE.*

art from faraway lands. They even billed themselves as a pilgrimage site with all their fancy relics. For centuries after, Venice stole relics to enhance their city, and doges used the stolen loot as propaganda.

With the sacking of Constantinople, the Venetians had destroyed much of their old way of life, so they had to build a new one. The Byzantines had been their best trading partner; now they had to trade more aggressively with others, which expanded their business and their reach. The Fourth Crusade forced Venice to build itself a new identity, and it used the stolen loot to make it a grand one.

Now, Venice could be an empire.

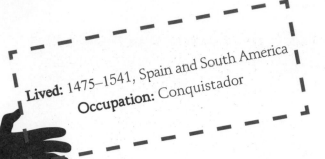

Francisco Pizarro

The Deadly Quarterback

Sticky Fingers

Spaniards in the sixteenth century were not great neighbors. Ever since **Christopher Columbus** sailed to the New World (the American continents) and yelled "mine!" they made it a habit to keep popping up uninvited and claiming they now owned the place.

They weathered storms, shipwrecks, and scurvy for lots of reasons, but there was always one constant: gold fever. The king of Spain first said to Columbus, "Get gold, humanely if possible, but at all hazards—get gold!"

Christopher Columbus:

He was from Italy, but worked for Spain.

Except there were already people living in the "new" world who owned the gold, and they weren't thrilled with their sticky-fingered new neighbors. Especially when the Europeans started torturing, killing, and enslaving them to find more gold.

Francisco Pizarro wasn't the first conquistador from Spain. He wasn't even the most famous conquistador from Spain. That dubious honor goes to Hernando Cortez, who destroyed the Aztecs in Mexico. But Pizarro might have been the most successful—his theft of Inca gold and silver transformed both the New World and the Old. These original conquistadors all followed the cardinal rule of conquering: there are no rules. But there was a playbook and Pizarro was one of the deadliest quarterbacks to use it.

"Pozing" Pizarro

Playbook to Conquering

The conquistadors' playbook didn't start with Hernando Cortez, but he made it famous by being super successful and inspiring Pizarro. With a band of five hundred men and all the right moves, he planned to invade present-day Mexico, sniff out all its gold, and crown himself a mini-king. Here's how he did it.

First: Make the invasion seem legal. Formally read the Requirement aloud in Spanish to the uncomprehending natives. The Requirement states that the natives are graciously donating their land to the king of Spain and surrendering peacefully. Otherwise, they will be killed. Their choice!

Second: Get approval from the king back home. This is done by proving the land is of value—it has gold and prospective slaves.

Third: Find gold.

Fourth: Get slaves.

Fifth: Make one of your slaves learn Spanish and interpret the native language for you.

Sixth: Puff yourself up to look really dangerous by parading horses and dogs and shooting guns—all of which natives have never seen—and killing a few hundred unarmed natives to get your point across.

Seventh: Kidnap the local king.

Eighth: Send the king of Spain the *quito*, his portion of gold. He gets a fifth of all your treasure, because he's the king.

Ninth: Enjoy the rest of all your fabulous wealth, natives not included!

Second Child Syndrome

illegitimate:

His parents weren't married, and according to the standards of the time, this meant Pizarro wasn't supposed to exist.

History doesn't know much about Pizarro's early life, except that he was always coming in second. Even though he was his father's oldest son, he was **illegitimate**. His father acknowledged all his other sons, except for Francisco. This meant Francisco was destined to be a pig farmer his whole life with no money, no aristocratic title, and no hope. But like his distant cousin Cortez, Pizarro had major get-up-and-go ambition, which led him to hop a ship to the New World to change his destiny.

Pacific Ocean:

The commander of the expedition, Vasco Núñez de Balboa, gets the credit for being the first European to spot the ocean. Pizarro got him back later by arresting and executing him under the king's orders.

Before he became the man who decimated an empire, Pizarro had already made some *almost* textbook-worthy accomplishments, like being the second European to spot the **Pacific Ocean**, and conquistadoring all over South America. He'd gone from rags to riches and could retire to his private island off the coast of Panama with all his money and slaves, but that wasn't enough for him. Even a share in a gold mine wasn't enough. Glittering dreams of more gold and more power kept him from being happy.

Recon

harquebuses:

Invented in the fifteenth century, a harquebus was the really slow father of the rifle. It was super dangerous to the user and sort of dangerous to the target with its long loading times, tripods, and tendency to explode.

At the age of forty-four, Pizarro was way over the hill and halfway down the other side—at least by sixteenth-century Spanish standards. If he wanted fame and fortune, he needed to get moving and find an empire to decimate. But while he had very little time to spare, Pizarro wasn't stupid. He knew better than to go into unexplored lands **harquebuses** blazing.

First, he led two expedi-
tions to scope out the area
known as Peru. It had a lot of
mountains.

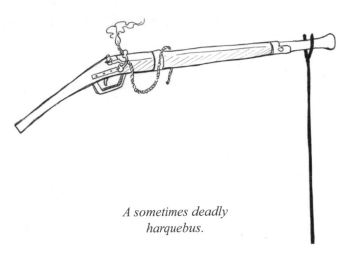

In both expeditions,
Pizarro got as close to disaster
as a person can get without
dying. During one, Pizarro's
expedition partner, Diego de
Almagro, lost an eye in a battle with natives, and in the

A sometimes deadly harquebus.

other, a bunch of men starved to death. Pizarro kept both his eyes on the prize
after stumbling across a raft filled with natives and their gold. They were on
a trading mission for the advanced civilization in the area—the Inca Empire.
Pizarro took everything on the raft, including the two native boys he forced
to learn Spanish so they could interpret for him.

Once Pizarro established that there was
gold in the area, he needed to visit the
king of Spain in person and convince
him there was tons more gold, just
around the mountain bend. Luckily
for Pizarro, **Charles V**'s gold fever
was as high as Pizarro's. He said yes
and gave Pizarro a few fancy titles.

Supporting Pizarro wasn't a
hard decision for Charles, who burned
through gold like straw and was always in
debt. A new fountain of treasures was exactly
what the king ordered to cure his gold fever.

Charles V:

It takes a lot of money to be
a king and even more to be an
emperor. Before he had gold from
the Americas, he'd borrowed a lot
to bribe his way into getting the
fancy-schmancy title of Holy Roman
Emperor (which was neither holy,
Roman, nor an empire—but it looked
good on a resume).

With his four half-brothers, his expedition partner Almagro, sixty-two
horses, and an assortment of 168 other pipe players, barbers, tailors, stone-
masons, and even a few enslaved Muslim women, Pizarro rode off to find
more fortune.

Fewer than two hundred non-warriors doesn't sound like good odds against an empire, but Pizarro also had the conquistadors' playbook and a lot of luck. Pizarro had already double-crossed Almagro by not bringing him back any fancy titles, and he was puffed up enough to think he was invincible. He wasn't done double-crossing people.

Pizarro marched over the Andes Mountains into an empire that was almost a million square miles. It wasn't that the current emperor, Atahualpa (ah-tah-WAL-pa), didn't know they were there—he had plenty of spies and messengers keeping him informed. Atahualpa simply allowed the Spaniards to keep marching because he was puffed-up, too. Mostly because the Inca were in the middle of a civil war, which Atahualpa was winning.

The civil war was because of Hernando Cortez's expedition into the Aztec

Empire a decade before. Disease travels faster than humans, and thanks to the walking petri dishes (Cortez's conquistadors), the previous Inca emperor had died of smallpox carried by the Europeans—even though he had never met any. His death left a power vacuum that his two sons were fighting to fill. Atahualpa had just captured his brother to win the battle, but Pizarro was determined to win their war.

Double-time!

Not a Fun Party

The nice Inca roads through the mountains were built for llamas, not horses, and the high elevation was making Pizarro's men sick. From his handy interpreters and the few residents he'd tortured for information about Atahualpa, Pizarro was starting to get the picture; conquering the Inca wasn't going to be easy. Finally, after twenty-one rough, cold, hard-to-breathe days on the march, Pizarro and his men straggled into what looked like an alien-advanced city: Cajamarca. Luckily for Pizarro, Atahualpa was in a curious, rather than murderous, mood. He also wasn't in town. He was a few miles away, relaxing in the area's natural hot springs.

It had begun to hail, and Pizarro didn't want to make a wrong move, so he sent his commander **Hernando de Soto** and fifteen horsemen to ask the emperor what to do. The emperor acted unimpressed. He ignored them completely and kept relaxing surrounded by a bunch of his girlfriends.

Hernando de Soto:

Soto would go on to use his share of the Inca treasure to conquer Florida. Instead of finding another gold-filled empire, he found the Mississippi River and death-by-fever.

Pizarro had a sudden "What was I thinking?" moment and hurriedly sent his brother and twenty more horsemen. Atahualpa was a little more interested to hear from the leader's brother. Even though the Spaniards broke just about every Inca rule, including looking directly at Atahualpa, he agreed to meet up with Pizarro in Cajamarca the following day. Neither expected it to be a party, although they both dressed up for the occasion.

Maybe Pizarro planned to roll with the punches and think up new strategies on the spot, but he had a back-up plan right out of the conquistadors' playbook: kidnap the head honcho. He not-so-discreetly stationed heavily armed men in the low buildings around the square, which definitely looked like a trap.

Atahualpa came dressed to impress in silver and gold, emeralds, and parrot feathers. He brought five or six thousand lightly armed men to parade around him. The sight of all these riches on display made some of the conquistadors drool in anticipation, but the sight of hundreds-to-one odds made a few others pee their armor in terror. There were tens of thousands more armed Inca warriors waiting outside the city, and no knew what the other side was really going to do.

Safe in his hidey-hole house, Pizarro first sent out a few guys and a priest to speak for him. Atahualpa sat watching from high above in a carried chair, possibly planning to kill the invaders afterward and then take their exotic horses to breed and then use to scare his enemies.

Not the beginning of a beautiful friendship.

The Spanish didn't want to waste time playing party. They asked the emperor to come down and talk. When he refused, the Spanish read the Requirement, which was a doctrine from the king of Spain, asking the natives to submit to Spanish rule—or die. Then, a Spanish Catholic friar held up his prayer book and said it would explain everything.

Atahualpa, never having seen writing before, was irritated by the weird squiggles on paper and the disrespect the conquistadors were showing. He threw their stupid book to the ground. That was all the insult Pizarro needed to sound the alarm. Screaming "Santiago!" the conquistadors attacked to the boom of cannons.

Santiago:

Saint James, or Santiago in Spanish, was a common battle cry when the Spanish fought, and a lot scarier when said while waving a sword with fanatical light gleaming in one's eyes.

Now, only the Spanish were having fun at this get-together. The Inca were terrified of the creepy monsters (horses) and the loud blasts of gunpowder. Eyewitnesses say they climbed on top of each other trying to get away, and many died from suffocation. The ones holding up Atahualpa's chair refused to let go; even after having their hands and arms cut off, they held up their emperor with their shoulders.

Pizarro charged through the massacre and grabbed Atahualpa from his armless guards. With their emperor captured, the whole kingdom was captured.

The Ultimate Double-Cross

Atahualpa had seen better days, like the day before when he'd been winning his civil war. Now, he was surrounded by bearded strangers who wanted his money. Seeing how feverish the Spaniards were about treasure, he offered to fill a **room** once with gold and twice with silver. All he wanted in exchange was his life.

room:

22 feet x 17 feet x 8 feet

Pizarro agreed to the deal. No word on if he stroked his beard in glee.

For seven months, caravans of llamas carried riches to the room. Pizarro passed the time by teaching Atahualpa how to play chess and firing up the forges. It didn't matter how beautiful the Inca artwork was; Pizarro threw almost all of it into the fire. He melted down $270 million worth of treasure and saved one oxcart-worth of artwork to send back to Spain. Charles V didn't care about the artwork, either, and threw the stolen treasures into his own forges ASAP.

As for Atahualpa, he was way too important to let go, and he would never have agreed to being a puppet king. After one super-fake trial where Atahualpa was convicted of rallying his army against the invaders, Pizarro sentenced him to burn at the stake—unless he converted to Christianity. Atahualpa promised to get more gold and silver if Pizarro would just take it and go back to Spain already, but Pizarro wasn't interested in striking another deal.

Since the Inca believed the dead were really still alive, just hanging out inside their mummified bodies, Atahualpa sort of wanted to keep his eternal body away from flames. He quickly "converted" and was baptized with Pizarro's name. Only minutes later, Pizarro's men strangled him to death.

Pizarro had to explain himself to his own king, Charles V, after that. When he sent a letter justifying the killing of Atahualpa, not even Charles bought Pizarro's story, and he sent a strongly worded letter to the thief about killing kings.

Treasure Seekers Beware

It's not just sixteenth century conquistadors who were obsessed with gold. Tales of lost Inca treasure persist today. Legend has it, there was one last payment of treasure due to the Ransom Room before Pizarro killed Atahualpa. When the Inca treasure-carriers heard about their king's death, they didn't hand over the booty with a forced smile; they hid it in a mountain cave. Ha!

Ever since, it's been a wild-silver-and-gold-and-emeralds chase through the Andes. The few people who claimed to have found it mysteriously died en route to riches. To this day, treasure seekers hope to find more cities like Cuzco covered in the shiny stuff and even the lost ransom treasure.

The lone remaining Inca building is called the Ransom Room,
but it's probably where Atahualpa was kept prisoner.

Not Going Down without a Fight

Pizarro sent his men to Cuzco, another sophisticated Inca city, where even the buildings were covered in gold. The conquistadors crowbarred the stuff right off the walls, including sacred Inca temples. Each plate of gold from the wall was close to five pounds and worth what the conquistadors would have had to work nine years to earn in their old jobs as sailors. They ripped off seven hundred gold plates from one temple alone. They couldn't carry all their loot by themselves, so they kidnapped one thousand natives and made their new slaves carry the treasure back to Pizarro in Cajamarca.

For appearances, Pizarro crowned a new Inca emperor. He was hoping to keep rebellions at bay and to collect taxes from the ten million Inca residents. The Spaniards also demanded the Inca tell them the location of more treasure. The Incas got the hint: these bearded strangers would never be content. Instead of rolling over and dying, they decided to fight back.

siege:

The Incas ended their siege thanks to Pizarro and Almagro's reinforcements, but the rebellion lasted more than thirty years throughout Peru!

At one point, the puppet king snuck out from under Spanish noses and gathered an army. For almost a year, the Incas laid **siege** to Cuzco. If it weren't for the thousands of natives on the Spanish side, the conquistadors would have been *toast-a-dors*. Pizarro quickly sent out a "Mayday! We're going down!" alarm to Spain, asking for reinforcements, which he got. Charles V had no intention of losing his endless fountain of silver and gold.

In the end, the rebellion didn't stand a chance. Pizarro & Co. were able to draw on too many tricky moves in the conquistador playbook. Pizarro survived long enough to gain a toehold in Peru thanks to steel swords, deadly diseases, and native allies.

Just the Beginning

The conquistadors didn't take their treasure and leave. They set up colonies, located a silver mine, and forced the natives to work for them, all while shipping back boatloads of money to Spain. In their wake, they left behind only ten percent of the native population. Europe, on the other hand, was in for a treat—to their taste buds. Along with the gold, conquistadors brought back new foods like chocolate, corn, potatoes, and tomatoes, forever changing Spain's culinary landscape.

In order to safely transport all that treasure across the Atlantic Ocean, Spain grouped their treasure ships together in big floating conveys called flotillas that set sail from the Spanish Main. Soon, Spain would be the dominant world power, driven by stolen gold. But like most ill-gotten gains, the good times didn't last forever.

The Spanish Main: A pirate's paradise.

Even with an unending supply of silver and gold and natives to mine it, Spain was better at spending than saving. Charles was pretty sure that being the best meant spending the most, and he left behind a debt large enough to send a man to the moon. He was constantly waging war (expensive) and getting his stolen money filched by greedy middlemen and pirates (rude). This included one very brazen thief named Queen Elizabeth I (see chapter 3). New World wealth ended up everywhere in the world, except in Spain, impacting and shaping economies with its golden touch.

As for Pizarro, he definitely died rich, but not asleep in his bed, and he never went back to Spain. That first double-cross against his partner ended up stabbing him in the back—literally.

After taking more than his fair share of the ransom, Pizarro founded the modern-day capital of Peru: Lima. Sure, he named it "City of Kings," claiming it was for the king of Spain, but he was the one wearing the crown.

Almagro simmered in anger as Pizarro flaunted his power and wealth.

In fact, Pizarro and Almagro were constantly squabbling over who got the bigger share. They clearly hadn't learned anything from the civil war among the Inca. Their personal problems with each other morphed into full-out war with Spaniards lining up on either side. They traded assassinations; Almagro went down first. Pizarro felt pretty confident—until a group of guys stabbed him while he was having dinner in his kingly city. All the money in the world couldn't save him from a bunch of knives in his back.

In less than ten years, Pizarro managed to decimate the Inca empire, used his city-building skills to create modern-day Peru, and helped finance Spanish wars that would change the course of history. His conquest of the New World began the "Modern Age," and the conquistadors' stolen riches caused Europe to boom economically and literally—there were only nine years of peace in sixteenth-century Europe. Still, a hundred ducats says Pizarro was probably only interested in his share of the spoils.

Memorize That!

Cajamarca, the first city Pizarro and his men entered, was scarily impressive. The conquistadors realized pretty quickly how advanced the Inca civilization was after seeing paved roads and the water (hot and cold!) they piped into their baths. The Incas didn't have the wheel, any type of writing, or arches in their architecture, but not even a knife could slide between the stones in the walls they built.

Instead of writing, they passed messages and kept track of records by knotting colorful ropes, called *quipus*. The colorful knots served as memory aides to tell stories, and also helped them remember how much quinoa they'd traded for alpaca wool. They used runners sprinting up and down the Andes mountains between cities to relay messages contained in the *quipus*. The Spaniards didn't find *quipus* as impressive as historians do today, and they unfortunately burned most of them and the secrets they held. Archaeologists are hoping to find something that unlocks their secrets one day.

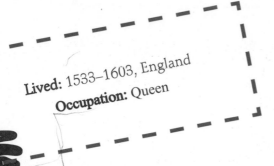

Lived: 1533–1603, England
Occupation: Queen

Chapter
3

Queen Elizabeth I of England

Busy Digesting the Spanish Armada

Not a Prince

Elizabeth was born a princess when everyone wanted her to have been born a prince. But she didn't let mere words stop her from sitting on the English throne or from reigning with the "heart and stomach of a king," as she liked to say. Rather than sitting around in pretty dresses and jewels all day whining about the unfairness of life, she sat around in pretty dresses and jewels and thieved her way to greatness.

Elizabeth had to act cold-blooded; her Protestant England was half of an already tiny island in a very Catholic Europe. If she wanted to keep her throne (and her head), she'd have to play smart and a little dirty. She didn't mind, especially if she could find someone else to do the actual dirty work.

Heart and stomach of a king?

A Lot of Marys but No One to Marry

When Elizabeth took the precarious English throne in 1559, lots of people didn't want her there. It wasn't just the Catholics of Europe; her own people questioned her ability. Threats against her life, failed assassinations, and attempted coups were as common as houseflies. And that doesn't even factor in the constant threat of a Spanish invasion thanks to her cousin Mary, Queen of Scots.

Mary, a Catholic, thought she should rule England as well as Scotland. King Philip II of Spain and the pope, two more Catholics, thought that was a great idea. Elizabeth obviously didn't agree. After nineteen years of disagreeing, Elizabeth chopped off Mary's head.

Bloodbath number one.

What Elizabeth didn't know was that Mary had secretly written a will hours before she died, declaring Philip the heir to the English throne. Philip definitely liked the sound of that.

Spain became an even bigger problem for Elizabeth. Philip took Mary's will to heart and kept floating the idea of a Spanish invasion. In his mind, England needed him, probably because he had been king of England for a while. He had married Elizabeth's older sister, a different **Mary**, and they had ruled like two Catholic peas in a pod. Until Mary died childless, Philip went back to Spain, and Elizabeth became queen.

Just to keep things weird, Philip offered to marry Elizabeth. She kept putting him off. Thanks, but no thanks. She claimed she had the heart of a man; she didn't need an actual man mucking things up and turning England back to Catholicism. Instead, Elizabeth got herself a different kind of man—one with no morals, no regard for human life, and nothing to lose. She got herself a pirate.

Mary:

The very Catholic Mary Tudor also didn't mind getting her hands bloody—people actually nicknamed her Bloody Mary for all the Protestants she sent to the stake (around three hundred).

Who wouldn't want me?

It's Not Stealing if You're a Queen

Francis Drake held the Spanish in the same regard as a rotten tooth. During his first command at sea, the Spanish attacked his ship, and Drake fled, embarrassing himself pretty badly in the process. He swore lifelong revenge on all Spaniards.

But Drake was no hero. His first mission included cruising down the coast of Africa, capturing and stuffing humans into his ships, and then sailing for two months across the Atlantic Ocean to the West Indies, where he sold those who hadn't died of starvation or disease on the voyage to Spanish plantation owners as slaves.

Technically, Philip had made it illegal for the Spanish colonies to trade with anyone but the Spanish, but Drake didn't care, and neither did Elizabeth. The slave trade was so profitable, Elizabeth gave Drake more ships to cram more Africans aboard to sell in the West Indies.

Bloodbath number two.

Drake learned a lot during this period, like how to be ruthless, how to lie to Spanish officials, how to plunder ships and villages, and how to threaten disobedient pirates by offering to blow them to Davy Jones's locker if they didn't shape up.

For a few years, Drake traded people for money and stole from whatever Spanish ships he came across. Sometimes, his eyes were too big for his ships, and he couldn't carry away all the Spanish silver he looted. (He buried it instead, which is how some historians believe tales of pirates burying treasure may have started.)

When Drake got back to England, Elizabeth didn't mind his pirating ways. She liked his style, and she really liked all the profit he made. For every £1 she invested in his fleet, he brought back £47, usually from the gold and silver he stole from Spanish ships returning from the New World.

This made Drake a privateer, which is a pirate who steals for a government. The Spanish just called him a nuisance and warned ports about El Draque—the dragon. The Spanish tried to outsmart English pirates by forming convoys—safety in numbers!—but the pirates soon developed faster ships to attack and outrun the Spanish galleons.

Philip was definitely irritated, now. Even more than when Elizabeth had snubbed his half-hearted marriage proposal. This was about his silver and gold!

galleons: big, heavy Spanish warships.

Around the World in 903 Days

In 1577, Elizabeth decided to secretly send the Dragon to the Pacific Ocean to find new trading sites. If he happened to find Spanish stuff to steal, then all the better. Drake couldn't wait for his trip—stealing was just another word for business in his dictionary.

Within a few months, all of Europe knew about Elizabeth's top secret plan. Even in a time without Internet or phones, gossip spread quicker than disease. Elizabeth didn't stop the expedition, though, and in December 1577, Drake sailed from Plymouth, England, along the coast of Africa, over to Brazil, down South America, and through the Strait of Magellan to the Pacific. This made him the first Englishman to enter the Pacific. He also claimed North America as an English colony. Of course, he pillaged and plundered **Spanish ships** and settlements like the pirate he was, but Elizabeth didn't mind.

Bloodbath number three.

Philip wanted to strangle the loud-mouthed privateer personally. He put a 20,000 ducat bounty on Drake's head. In today's money, that's about 24 million dollars. Elizabeth didn't care. Irritating Philip delighted her so much that she knighted Drake in 1581 for his pirating ways after he returned victorious from his voyage around the world. He was the second person after **Ferdinand Magellan** to circumnavigate the globe.

Elizabeth kept the exact amount of stolen treasure a secret, but it was certainly enough to buy her own country and name herself supreme ruler of it. It's estimated that 10–15 percent of the total Spanish treasure was looted by Elizabeth!

Spanish ships:

Like the treasure ship nicknamed Cacafuego, which literally means fire-poop. The Cacafuego had so much of Philip's gold and silver onboard when Drake raided it that it took Drake's crew six days to bring the treasure over to their ship.

Ferdinand Magellan:

Magellan didn't actually make it the whole way around the world. Thinking he was superior in every way to the locals, he died a grisly death in the Philippines after being shot with a poisoned arrow by a native. His crew sailed the rest of the way home without him, but he still gets credit.

Not bad for a poor boy turned thief.

The Spanish wanted some serious consequences for all the looted villages and burned churches Drake left in his wake. Elizabeth assured them that she was very embarrassed by this wild pirate, and that she would make sure that he'd be punished. Then she sent a message to Drake congratulating him and telling him not to worry about a thing.

After having him lie low for a couple of years, Elizabeth prepared to send Drake on another privateering mission against Philip in 1585. The only official orders she gave her favorite pirate was to retake the English ships Philip kept in his ports. Obviously, Drake was free to make general mayhem, but this way, Elizabeth could pretend he went rogue.

She'd loosed a rabid animal on the world, and Drake pressed into his service French and Spanish ships alike. The Dragon sailed through the Caribbean islands and around Florida, decimating Spanish settlements, plundering and burning them to the ground like the true monster he was. This trip wasn't as profitable as Drake and Elizabeth had hoped, but it was still a major blow to Philip's pride. He complained about Drake constantly, but everyone knew who he really thought of as the problem. If Philip wanted to take down the woman behind the pirate, he'd need all the gold and ships he could get.

By 1586, both England and Spain smelled war. Word on the street was that Philip wanted to capture Elizabeth and send her in chains to the pope. He promised that any Englishman over seven years old wouldn't survive a Spanish invasion. People in England were so terrified, they thought they saw Spanish ships landing everywhere that year, although none had. And everyone had an opinion—letters full of advice for Elizabeth flooded in. Even Drake offered his two cents: launch a full-frontal assault with lots of looting and burning, of course.

Elizabeth eventually agreed with her Dragon. In the spring of 1587, she sent Drake on another trip to Spain, but this was no vacation. Elizabeth gave him six of her own ships and allowed twenty-five other ships go along to help spread the rumor that they were headed to the usual treasure spots in the West Indies to pillage gold. Only the pillaging gold part was true.

Feeling on top of the world.

By the time the Spanish figured out whose ships were entering their port, it was too late. The Dragon breathed his fire all over the town of Cádiz, Spain. He captured provisions, burned ships, and stomped off to find his next victim. For over a month, Drake did his favorite thing in the world, and he was an equal opportunity demolisher. He burned everything from fishing boats to warships. Especially thrilling for Drake was capturing the king's own ship, the *San Felipe*, on its way home from India carrying spices, silks, treasure, and ivory. The *San Felipe* had so much cargo on it, the crew couldn't use its cannons to save themselves. Drake captured the ship and sailed home to Elizabeth, £114,000 richer.

With so much destruction, Spanish captains were afraid to leave harbor for a whole month. Messages went out to the West Indies to keep treasure ships there until Drake was done looting.

Drake set the Spanish invasion back a whole year with his antics. Provisions Philip needed to launch his invasion of England, like a ship's worth of barrel-making materials necessary for storing soldiers' food and water, were now swimming with the fishes. This gave Elizabeth more time to get her unprepared country ready for war, including putting a dragon in **command** of her navy.

> **command:**
> Well, second-in-command. The top admiral position had to go to someone a bit more highborn than Drake, for appearances' sake. Someone like Charles Howard, First Earl of Nottingham. But everyone knew who was in charge.

Battle Royal

Elizabeth and Philip were wary by nature, so at first, the great, history-altering battle was like watching two turtles duke it out: painfully slow with lots of breaks. Both monarchs were known for their restraint and changed their minds frequently about when and where to attack, or if they would attack at all.

No Time for Fun and Games

An invading hostile army is no joke, so Elizabeth didn't allow any. In fact, she called off all fun and games for her people until the threat was over. In 1580, she banned games and gambling (a very Elizabethan-era thing to do). If you were a boy between the ages of seven and seventeen, you had to own a bow and at least two arrows and learn how to use them. The popular game of bowls was off-limits, too, as well as tennis, dice, cards, or "any other manner of game . . . or any game new invented." So don't get cute and use your imagination or you might find yourself in jail.

Full rundowns of Spain's plans became common knowledge around Europe's gossipy courts, and by April 1588, Philip's newly named "Invincible Armada" was ready to sail into history. Philip knew as well as anyone else that the English ships were faster with longer guns. After all, he'd helped build up the English navy when he was married to Bloody Mary! But he still believed everything would work out for Spain, and he really wanted the dreaded **Spanish Inquisition** to take root in England. His subjects smuggled pamphlets into England that proclaimed English subjects were free from obeying Elizabeth. They should kill her instead and join the Spanish army.

Spanish Inquisition:

Anybody living in Spain who wasn't Catholic, including Jews and Muslims, hid while priests hunted them down, tortured them, and forced them to confess to heresy (religious beliefs differing from those of the Catholic Church). Philip also used the Spanish Inquisition to root out people who didn't like him.

But the Invincible Armada had problems from the start, including a three-week wait, courtesy of storms. The food stored in the new, quickly made barrels (courtesy of Drake's earlier destruction of the better-quality materials) spoiled. The men ate it anyway, but they all got sick and wished they'd starved instead. More freak storms in June scattered the navy and killed six thousand of Philip's men. By the time they limped into the English Channel, even a sea slug looked more "invincible" than the Spanish Armada.

bowls:

A game played outside where big balls (called bowls) are thrown toward one small ball (called a jack) in hopes of getting your bowls closest.

The English defenders had food and gunpowder shortage problems, too. When the two navies finally came face-to-face on July 31st, they both came hungry. Drake was engaged in a game of **bowls** when he was told that the Armada had arrived. He decided he had time to finish the game and still beat the Armada. It wasn't just big talk. He was also waiting for the tide to turn so that his ships could leave shore.

Though all of the events leading up to this moment had happened excruciatingly slowly, the stage was finally set for the big showdown. Despite their recent setbacks, Spain was still considered to have the

History can wait! I'm winning.

greatest navy in the world, while upstart England only had their own navy thanks to Philip. During the first attack, both sides shocked each other. The English realized the Armada was tougher than beef jerky, while the Spanish were stunned by the new techniques the English employed—maneuvers that went against everything the books taught.

Each night, both sides took a bit of a breather. One night, Drake used the time to raid a Spanish ship of 50,000 ducats, instead of commanding his men. The English ships scattered without leadership and almost let the Spanish Armada land on English soil. Even worse, Drake stole on the job and only gave half of the ducats to Elizabeth. Once a pirate, always a pirate.

As daily battles raged on, the English kept surprising the Spanish, doing the complete opposite of what the more-seasoned navy anticipated. There was no jumping aboard enemy vessels and no hand-to-hand combat as expected; English ships sidled up to Spanish galleons and blasted the snot out of them one-by-one before sailing away to safety. It was *so* not gentlemanly. But Elizabeth was no gentleman. She was a woman, and she was winning.

For ten days, the navies bulldozed each other. After the smoke settled, the winner was clear. Thanks to lucky winds and a discarded rulebook, Elizabeth had bloodbath number four under her giant neck ruff. Philip had nothing.

You Sank My Battleship!

All the Spanish ships took at least some damage, and only a third of the men survived. Whole bloodlines were wiped out. Spain went into mourning. Court gossip turned to wondering how Spain would survive its worst loss in their history.

Elizabeth didn't lose any ships (she voluntarily set eight on fire to scare the Spanish and hopefully to burn some of their wooden ships to the water-line) and lost only 150 men, though lots of veterans died afterward due to lack of food and medicine. To the hundred soldiers that set the fireships ablaze, Elizabeth ponied up a measly £5—to share among themselves.

Meanwhile, Elizabeth decided she should smash in Philip's stupid, royal nose and finish him off once and for all. She sent Drake on another expedition in 1589 to end the Armada and bring back as much booty as possible. That failed, too, when Drake, as usual, went off-plan so he could raid other towns, giving Spanish ships plenty of time to escape his next attack.

For six years, Elizabeth refused to give him another command. Instead, over the next decade, she ordered 236 treasure-motivated attacks by other privateers. It wasn't until 1595 that she relented and sent Drake to raid Spanish colonies near Puerto Rico, which was too bad for the Dragon, because he died of dysentery during the trip.

Philip swore an oath to defeat Elizabeth no matter the cost, but he was pretty much crazed from

ROUTES OF THE ARMADA
✕ Fights in the channel
⚓ Wrecks

Well, that was a disaster.

grief at this point. He sent two more armadas in 1596 and 1597. Storms scattered them, sinking all but one of his battleships. Spain was no longer a world power, and England would never be Catholic nor face the Spanish Inquisition. Instead, Elizabeth became a legend, and the British navy dominated the seas for centuries.

If that sounds cool and you'd like to rule the waves, just remember: theft is only okay if it's the sixteenth century and you happen to be a queen with the stomach of a king.

Lived: 1729–1796, Russia
Occupation: Empress

Chapter
4

Catherine the Great

Loves a Good Coup

Making Luck

Catherine was a thinker. That's how she got to be "Great." And by taking whatever she wanted, of course. She was born a minor princess of nowhere, Germany, and she was destined to go nowhere fast. Rather than letting nothing be her fate, Catherine believed that "fortune is not blind." It favors the bold.

Nothing was bolder than stealing an empire.

Russian:

Peter III was the grandson of Peter the Great through his mother, but he grew up in Holstein, which was located in present-day Denmark and Germany.

Dear Diary

Catherine wasn't Russian, but in the game of musical European thrones, that wasn't a roadblock to becoming empress of Russia. At the tender age of fourteen, it was decided she would marry the heir to the Russian throne, her fifteen-year-old second cousin Peter. He wasn't Russian, either.

Ick factor aside, Peter and Catherine were not meant to be. Even though they were both German and close in age, she confided to her diary that he was stupid, ugly, childish, and didn't care for Russia at all. Unlike Peter, Catherine figured she'd better learn to love her new country.

While he played with toy soldiers, Catherine learned Russian, studied up on their new **religion**, and tried to play nice-future-wife.

religion:
The official religion of Russia was Russian Orthodox, a branch of Christianity that's still practiced in Russia today. Peter hated his forced baptism and tried to make Russia adopt Lutheran religious practices as emperor.

Catherine was determined to warm cold Russian hearts to her cause, and she claimed she even got pneumonia by practicing her Russian late at night while walking around without wearing enough layers to stay warm. The common people loved it; they walked around without enough layers, too!

She definitely wasn't warming her boyfriend's heart, though. When Peter got a case of smallpox, a disease that left his face full of scarred holes, he asked Catherine if she recognized him anymore. It was sort of a give-away when Catherine could only stammer her response. She wrote to her dear diary that he was, indeed, "hideous."

From then on, they both knew the deal. Catherine wanted to be empress, even if she had to kiss an ugly frog, over and over. The ugly frog was not hoppy.

That's Peter's good side.

Prussia:

Located in central and eastern Europe and covering a number of modern-day countries, including Germany and Poland. Prussia's capital was Berlin.

Who Needs Enemies When You Have Family?

Besides not getting to pick her happily ever after, Catherine also couldn't pick her family. Her only ally at the Russian court, her mother, Johanna, was spying for the king of **Prussia**, Frederick the Great. That was a problem, since her mother wasn't any good at it.

The current empress, Elizabeth of Russia, was hurt. She'd handpicked Catherine's family to marry her heir, not to spy on her. Elizabeth knew that as soon as Catherine was married to Peter and became empress, she could send Johanna away. Besides, Elizabeth was really impatient for those two crazy kids to get married. She needed them to give her a baby heir to continue the royal line. After Catherine's sweet sixteen, Empress Elizabeth dragged her down the wedding aisle.

By the time the last piece of wedding cake went stale, Elizabeth had also packed Johanna's bags. Although Johanna didn't leave without giving one last gift: a huge debt that would take Catherine seventeen years to pay off. Thanks, Mom!

Prussia is not Russia with an extra letter.

Elizabeth was only interested in one thing from Catherine and that was an heir ASAP. Nothing about Catherine was private, especially not her private life.

To make sure the un-lovebirds completed their task, Elizabeth assigned a new **maid** to lock the couple in their room at night. The maid took her job very seriously and insisted that Catherine did, too. Catherine couldn't joke around with her maids, and any that were too friendly were fired. Having friends was not in the baby-making job description. Catherine's new life at the Russian royal court was like jail, but with diamonds and better food.

maid:
Forget the toilet brush. These maids were noblewomen who hung out with queens and princesses all day as companions for the honor of serving royalty. It was a powerful position to hold in court.

Her overbearing new family made her miserable, but to Catherine, Peter was the worst of them all. She said he was "as discreet as a cannon" and only two weeks after the wedding, he told her he was in love with someone else.

Unhappy Wife, Unhappy Life

Peter flipped and flopped in and out of love, but never with his wife. He spent most of his time playing with toy soldiers and making his servants drill with muskets, as though they were Prussian soldiers. For Peter, it was all Prussia all the time. While Russia and Prussia sound similar, the two countries were very different. In fact, they were technically at **war**! Powerful Russians were concerned Peter didn't care for their country and would end the war when he became emperor. Catherine took notes on how not to behave: don't even joke about making friends with Prussia around the Russians.

war:
The Seven Years' War was fought with Prussia and Britain on one side and France, Russia, Austria, and a whole bunch of other, smaller countries on the other. It even spilled over to the American colonies, making it a global war.

In his spare time, Peter enjoyed some questionable hobbies. He hanged a rat he'd enlisted in his toy army for the crime of "eating papier-mâché sentries," spied on Elizabeth through little holes he drilled in the wall, and "trained" hunting dogs by letting them live in his bedroom and use it as a bathroom.

This was unfortunate for Catherine's nostrils, but even worse for her nose was Peter. He believed baths were dangerous to his health. And since there was no baby, there was no escape. The pair was forced to hang out all the time.

Finally, nine years after Catherine and Peter got married, Elizabeth got her baby heir. Catherine's duty was done. Now she could spend her time doing what she really wanted—being ambitious. She used her money and wits to make political alliances. She even turned a few of her former jailors to her side. Except Peter. He was really good at holding a grudge.

Sole Survivor

When Elizabeth died in 1762, Peter became emperor. His glorious reign lasted six months. That was all the time Catherine decided she wanted to wait.

Peter had been talking nonstop about his wanting a new wife, Catherine's going to live in a convent, and Prussia, Prussia, Prussia. He was even passing Russian secrets to Frederick the Great! When Peter finally became emperor, he gave Frederick Russian land, ended the war with Prussia, and made all of his soldiers wear tight-fitting Prussian uniforms. Nobody was happy but Peter.

Peter also took control of Russian churches and made them do as he said. They couldn't own land and had to pay taxes on their peasants. Now the army and the church were upset with Peter.

Even though he'd ticked off just about everyone, Peter wasn't worried about Catherine doing anything drastic. She kept playing possum, making him think she was weak whenever he ordered her around or ignored her completely, which was a big snub. Really, she was just laying the groundwork to get rid of him—for good.

If Peter did something stupid, like make that treaty with Prussia, she made sure the court and even foreign ambassadors knew she hated Prussia. When he humiliated her in front of the court by parading around his new girlfriend, Catherine only had to look sad and stay silent to gain instant popularity points. Secretly, she was feeling out her support and bringing important military leaders in Russia to her cause. She bided her time, waiting for Peter to make one more mistake.

Then he started a meaningless war with Denmark.

The moment Peter left town to play war, Catherine and her allies decided to drop the act. This was a **coup d'état** (coo day-TAH), and afterward Catherine was cooing with delight. That's because, on June 28th, 1762, she and forty of her closest friends took over St. Petersburg.

coup d'état:
A fancy French word for overthrowing a ruler.

Forty friends calling you queen was great, but Catherine needed an army if she was going to keep her new throne. She talked to all the soldiers left in the capital who hated the tight uniforms. They kissed her hands, shouted "Yes!" to her rousing speeches about saving Russia from the monster, and rode to a cathedral to have the Archbishop proclaim her empress. Then they tore off their Prussian uniforms and put on their comfy, old ones.

The only loose end was Peter. He was still technically emperor. In order to force him to give up the throne, Catherine figured she had to make him see the light—personally. A few soldiers gave her bits and pieces of their uniforms until she was wearing her own. She hopped on a big, white horse and marched out of the capital with fourteen thousand really pumped-up soldiers behind her to find and arrest Peter.

CATHERINE II. SUPPORTED BY THE ARMY AT ST. PETERSBURG.

Empress-in-Shining-Armor

Peter thought his wife was spending the day getting ready for a party in his honor in their second palace, right outside of St. Petersburg, just like he'd ordered her to do. When he went there, he found her party dress laid out on the bed without her in it. Word got out that she was on the march.

Peter laughed when his advisors told him to flee to fight another day. It wasn't until he tried to show himself to some of his men, and they responded by saying, "We no longer have an emperor!" that Peter realized things were capital-N Not Good. He started crying and wrote Catherine a letter, promising to share half of the throne with her. For Catherine, it was too little, too late. She responded to his letter by marching quicker.

Peter wrote a second letter, this time **abdicating** and begging to be left alive.

abdicating:
giving up one's throne.

Catherine accepted, but she still had him arrested. Adding insult to injury, his idol, Frederick the Great, commented that Peter, "allowed himself to be dethroned like a child being sent to bed."

Peter became a political prisoner. He also became a problem. Catherine sent him to their summer estate, where he sat around doing nothing. This arrangement felt pretty threatening to Catherine. What if someone decided they hated her and rallied around him? The best situation would be for Peter to fall asleep and never wake up.

Eight days later, Catherine's mind-reading musclemen strangled Peter with a scarf. (That was after they tried to suffocate him with a mattress, from which he wriggled free.) Was Catherine aware of the soldiers' plan? No one knows. Either way, dead is dead.

In the Driver's Seat

Catherine was now in charge, but that didn't mean she could spend her days swimming in a pool of jewels. She had to prove herself. Luckily, she was a "people person."

To keep the army and church on her side, she corrected many of Peter's unpopular decisions, including reversing the edict that soldiers had to wear tight Prussian uniforms, ending the war with Denmark, and returning land to the church.

Even so, Catherine liked some of Peter's ideas. In less than two years since starting her reign, she brought the church more firmly under her control, closing 411 of 572 churches. By that time, she was so popular that no one made a peep. She even made an alliance with Frederick and Prussia, but she made it seem like a great idea. Anything Peter *thought* he could do, Catherine did better.

Enlightened:

A movement in the eighteenth century called "the Enlightenment" emphasized science and rational thinking.

When her advisors suggested sparing her the tedious task of paperwork, Catherine politely declined. Unlike Elizabeth and Peter, she didn't intend to be a backseat ruler. She'd drive the country herself, on the Enlightened side of the road.

To Catherine, ruling with an Enlightened fist just made sense. An Enlightened ruler was in charge, but they also wanted to help the little people. Enlightened rulers reformed the government according to Enlightenment principles—like giving peasants more rights.

How'd that get there?

To be considered Enlightened by the rest of Europe, Catherine first had to prove she wasn't a bloodthirsty tyrant who'd killed her husband in cold blood. Or killed another claimant to the throne who'd died in a jail cell under questionable circumstances. Or killed a few nasty, rebellion-starting folks who kept claiming they were Peter. Beheadings hurt her Enlightened street cred, but that was the only way she felt she could deal with traitors.

So Catherine made a few philosopher friends who were pretty big in the Enlightened world. They were supposed to tell the rest of Europe how enlightened she was, too. To keep Europe talking about her, she bought Diderot's library of books and then paid him to be her librarian (see Ringside). She wanted artists, writers, and scientists to flock to Russia, which they did.

Catherine left the nurturing of her children to the nanny, and nursed other things, like the arts.

> ### Ringside
>
> Catherine didn't want to be a lightweight in the Enlightenment, so she hung out with the heavyweights, hoping some of their influence would rub off on her. Here are some of her sparring partners (aka pen pals), and their contributions:
> - **Denis Diderot:** wanted to put all the world's knowledge in one place, so he wrote the thirty-two-volume *Encyclopédie*.
> - **Voltaire:** wrote the humorous book *Candide*, which made fun of many of the political, religious, and philosophical systems of the day.
> - **Madame Geoffrin:** hosted *salons*, or hangouts, where smart people talked about untouchable stuff all day, like freedom and tradition.

She started an art museum by rounding up famous paintings before anyone else could, and made herself the leading art collector in Europe. There was no better way to leave her mark than to do so literally—with really big buildings. Catherine embraced architecture, calling herself "addicted," and had a museum built for her paintings. Named the Hermitage Museum, it still stands in Saint Petersburg today where it is continually ranked as one of the best museums in the world.

Education was super important to the Enlightenment, and Catherine agreed. How could Russia ever be as great as she was if no one could read? How could they ever love Russia if they didn't learn about the importance of **civic** duty?

civic: public.

Catherine ordered a few men to study European schools and report back with a plan for Russian education. She created boarding schools for orphans, like those seen in England, where they could learn a trade, like carpentry. Then she opened a women-only college and made the president a woman, too. She was setting the example for women in charge—a revolutionary idea in the eighteenth century.

Europe was definitely talking.

No Rest Stops

Catherine wasn't ready to rest on her Enlightened laurels. She wanted a new set of laws for her new land, and she wanted those laws to align with Enlightenment ideals. After reading all of her favorite philosophers, she wrote up her own how-to guide complete with over five hundred bullet points. She plagiarized a lot, but she admitted that.

Called the *Nakaz*, it was everything Catherine wanted in her new code of law, including pompous ideas like outlawing torture, and that all men are created equal (nine years before Thomas Jefferson wrote the Declaration of Independence). Those irresponsible ideas led countries like France to ban the *Nakaz*. The French king didn't want any of that sort of talk stirring up ideas in his **loyal subjects**.

loyal subjects:

His "loyal" subjects later beheaded his son, King Louis XVI, and daughter-in-law, Marie Antoinette, for not making them feel equal enough.

When she was done, Catherine called together people from each region, from peasants to aristocrats, to write up a new set of laws for the country. Catherine wanted to make a more productive Russia, but she made the mistake of giving everyone too much of a say. Since the delegates couldn't agree on anything, not a single law was written.

absolutely:

An absolute monarch is a ruler who is not bound by any rules or regulations. Nobody told Catherine how to rule.

Catherine learned a valuable lesson: she should **absolutely** be the only one in charge. Otherwise, nothing would ever get done, and

Catherine most certainly did not steal a throne for nothing.

When her law dreams flopped, Catherine found other ways to help the little people. She set up a school for doctors and established hospitals in every province.

Next, Catherine wanted to combat disease. At a time when people blamed doctors for illness, she ordered a vaccination against small-pox for herself and the second most important person in Russia—her son. When they both survived, it sent a pretty strong message. Nobles lined up to get smallpox shots.

The doctor who gave Catherine her smallpox shot on the right.

She also whipped the decrepit navy into shape, allowing Russia to destroy her enemies on land and sea. Her stunning victories were a bit terrifying to even her friends. They wondered how far she'd go. And they were right to. She scooped up Poland and marched through her neighbors, adding 200,000 square miles and pushing the **boundaries of Russia** farther than ever before.

boundaries of Russia:

Catherine the Great added much of modern-day Poland, Ukraine, and Crimea to Russia. This gave Russia access to the Black Sea, which was important for shipping and commerce!

How to Be Great

At the age of sixty-seven, the eighteenth century's version of a ripe old age, Catherine died from a stroke while sitting on the toilet. Even the greats have to do their business.

Catherine became a "Great" because she wasn't afraid to change the world with her ill-gotten gains. Peter became a dimwit because he lost, and losers don't get to tell their side of history.

Russia went from being the country other countries laughed at to being a world power. Europe realized Russia wasn't all bears and snowstorms, and it took notice of the new power on the continent. Arts and artists flourished and gave the world epic masterpieces like *War and Peace* and beautiful ballets about swans.

All thanks to Catherine.

Lived: 1769–1821, Europe

Occupation: General, Emperor, Revolution Killer

Napoleon Bonaparte

Art Critic in Training

First-Name-Only Kind of Guy

Napoleon was known for many things, like being **short**, wearing funny hats, and that whole world-domination thing. But he was a military genius who only lost seven battles out of sixty and created modern France in the process. Along the way, he made some mistakes, too—including selling land to the United States for less than three cents an acre in the Louisiana Purchase and the incident that was his downfall: losing the Battle of Waterloo, possibly thanks to a bad case of hemorrhoids. (Google it.)

short:

Actually, at 5'7", Napoleon's height was average for a Frenchman of the time, if not a teeny bit taller. It was his archnemeses, the British, who liked to poke fun by claiming he was short.

Louisiana Purchase: What a steal!

Still, it's Napoleon's thievery on an international scale that changed the world. It led to the appointment of the first modern museum director who organized the first modern museum. You may have heard of it. The Louvre is still one of the most famous museums today. Its illustrious standing is thanks to one guy who knew one important thing: pictures have power.

The Fanciest Museum on the Block

palace:

Before it was a palace, the building was a military fort. You can still visit the thirteenth-century stone ruins in the Lower Hall of the Louvre.

liberté, égalité, fraternité:

French for liberty, equality, and fraternity (brotherhood). It's still the national French motto.

Before the Louvre became one of the most-visited museums in the world, it was a **palace**. French kings and queens lived there with an impressive collection of art from Old Masters and young pups (contemporary artists—or, at least, contemporary at the time). Two days a week, the royals let citizens drink in the paintings' beauty. Otherwise, it was closed to the regular Joes and Josephines.

Then the French Revolution swept Paris, and the regular people decided the snooty, well-born aristocrats had to go—and not into retirement. Royal heads rolled off royal bodies, including the king and queen's. The new government had to figure out what to do with all the fancy palaces and pretty pictures the dead aristocrats had left behind. It only seemed right to give the cultural riches to the people as a symbol of *liberté, égalité, fraternité!*

The revolutionaries arrested the king, and nine days later, they declared that art would be "the most powerful illustration of the French Republic."

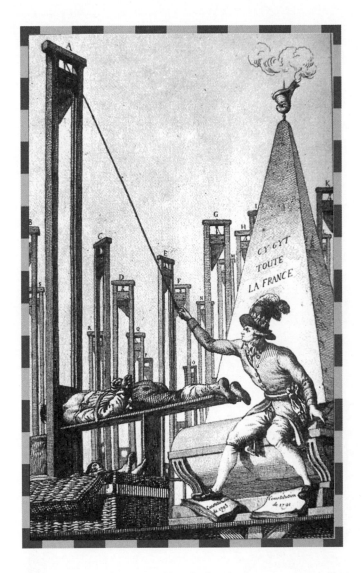

It's impossible not to lose your head when looking up at a guillotine.

Preserving the left-behind art was almost their first priority, which says a lot for a revolution that eventually guillotined fifty thousand people.

Since there was already a plan in place to turn part of the Louvre into a museum, the revolutionaries decided to stick with that idea. They opened the Louvre to the public free of charge, offering over six hundred works for their viewing pleasure.

The whole place was a rat's nest of pictures, sculptures, vases, clocks, and other unlabeled works of art that had been thrown onto the walls like paint splatter. The museum was an illegible assortment of styles and years, grouped together only by color scheme. But its lack of order wasn't its only problem. The Louvre also had a lot of structural issues, and it was closed after only three years.

It would take one ambitious man to reopen the museum in a grander fashion than ever before. And he didn't care much for art. Napoleon cared about one thing: his reputation. As his advisors told him, art was *très important* to the French, so it became *très important* to Napoleon.

Napoleon vs. The World

Looting was a well-established practice long before Napoleon stomped his way across Europe taking what he liked (see chapter 1). If you were leading a conquering army, you let your men take whatever wasn't bolted down as spoils of war and called it part of their paycheck.

Napoleon could conquer cities, letting his men loot like armies had been doing since the dawn of time . . . or he could cherry-pick the best stuff to send back to Paris, which would make *everyone* in France (and not just his army) love him.

Napoleon couldn't care less about the **contrapposto** of the *Apollo Belvedere* or the triumphs achieved by Renaissance genius Raphael, but his advisors convinced him that keeping the art for the French people to enjoy was the best political move. *Vive la France!*

contrapposto:

The pose artists give to humans to reflect shifting weight. The Ancient Greeks (and their Roman copiers) were masters of this lifelike technique. The Apollo Belvedere is a Roman copy.

The first step for Napoleon was figuring out what was worth taking during his Italian campaign. A team of experts, including a botanist, a chemist, a few artists, and an archaeologist tagged along on raids to choose the best items Italy had to offer. They identified artistic works and manuscripts based on how famous and how rare they were. Their job was to strip Italy of the title of "capital of the art world," and give it to Paris.

Oh look, more art! - Apollo Belvedere, probably

Pretending to act legally, Napoleon didn't do a smash and grab. He drew up contracts offering peace in exchange for cash and art. After facing Napoleon's lightning-fast army, people chose peace.

The Duke of Parma was first. He had to cough up twenty paintings. Bologna gave thirty-one paintings and almost six hundred manuscripts. Venice lost her famous horses, twenty paintings, and five hundred manuscripts. The pope was the saddest of all. He had to contribute a hundred masterpieces (mostly ancient marble sculptures) and the entire papal archive of historical documents to Napoleon's grand plan for glory.

Napoleon took his flair for showmanship and leveled it up. He couldn't just load all his new statues and paintings onto a horse-drawn carriage and ship them to Paris quietly! Throwing a party was a much better plan. It was a nightmare trying to figure out how to transport the art anyway, so why not turn it into a cross-continent extravaganza and keep everyone's attention on him?

I'll miss you!

Everyone in Paris celebrated the arrival of the Roman treasures with a parade that included a display of troops, specially composed music, caged lions, and, of course, art. Huge convoys of buffalo and oxen pulled carts across mountain ranges to the coast. It was a grand spectacle, just like Napoleon wanted. It was also incredible that all of the fragile marble statues from ancient Greece and Rome didn't fall off a ravine and break into millions of pieces.

The parade enabled Napoleon to show the French people his power in a concrete way. Instead of hearing secondhand reports or taking the newspapers at their word, citizens could see with their very own eyes how successful Napoleon had been. Celebratory vases and commemorative coins were created to reinforce his message: Paris was on top and Napoleon had been the one to get her there.

But Napoleon didn't wait around to be showered with praise. He didn't even show up for the parade. He'd had already planned his next war and was on his way to Egypt with even more experts in tow.

You know what they say: go big or go home.

Not Here for Sightseeing

The team of experts Napoleon brought with him to Egypt in 1798 made his Italian crew look like finger-painting preschoolers. That's because he brought 167 *savants* and his personal library of 125 manuscripts along for the trip.

Napoleon marched his men across blazing hot deserts, fought battles alongside ancient pyramids, and suffered some serious setbacks, including the time the British destroyed his navy during the Battle of the Nile. But art-wise,

savants:

smarty-pants thinkers including scientists, engineers, and scholars.

library:

Napoleon didn't know the meaning of "beach reads." He brought classics including works by Roman authors Livy and Plutarch, travel books from Captain Cook, and the Islamic holy book, the Koran, since Egypt was controlled by Muslim Ottomans at the time of his campaign, and he wanted to acquaint himself with their faith and laws before meeting with them. It's all about the winning angles for Napoleon!

The Battle of the Pyramids looks hot.

his *savants* did a pretty great job, and that's what the Napoleon-controlled newspapers focused on back home.

In order to bring the European way of thinking to Egypt, Napoleon opened up the Institute of Egypt in Cairo.Even though Napoleon wanted his *savants* to study things like ovens that were better at baking bread for his hungry army, the *savants* soon started researching things they wanted to learn about, including Egyptology, the study of ancient Egyptian culture, mummies definitely included.

One *savant*, artist Vivant Denon, endured military marches, bug bites, disease, sandstorms, and bumpy camel rides to write a grand account of their journey. Bullets regularly whistled past his ears, but Denon didn't stop sketching temple ruins for anything short of shooting back. Napoleon's campaign and Denon's book began a wave of Egyptomania across Europe, which is exactly what it sounds like—the craze for all things Egypt.

In the end, the Egyptian campaign was a bust since it gained Napoleon neither land nor power—his main objectives in life. All the great things he accomplished for the art world didn't matter to him if he couldn't control it.

After an outbreak of the plague, multiple defeats, and a general lack of supplies, Napoleon knew it was time to cut his losses. He secretly left Egypt for Paris, where he promptly overthrew the government and made himself a dictator.

The Thief and the Thief

In 1802, Napoleon named Denon director of the Louvre. It only took seven months for the museum to be renamed the Musée Napoleon—the Napoleon Museum.

Besides wanting the Musée Napoleon to be the most beautiful museum in the world, Denon wanted to make it one gigantic art history lesson. He tackled the unruliness by organizing the artwork, putting in skylights, expanding the galleries, and building a grand staircase. Denon used all the famous pieces collected during Napoleon's campaign for world domination to create his own curatorial masterpiece. Artifacts were no longer arranged by how well their colors complemented one another, but by artist, geographic locale, and school. Restoration of the artwork was handled by professionals.

Denon refused to become an armchair artist. He accompanied Napoleon on campaign after campaign, always searching for the best pieces for his museum. Combing through Italian monasteries, Denon picked up underappreciated "primitive" works from the period that we now call the proto-Renaissance, which enabled him to complete his art history lesson for the people of France. Following in the footsteps of the French army, Denon took so much art that the French generals referred to him as the "thief on the coattails of the Grand Army."

Don't let the velvet fool you— Denon could camel-ride with the best.

After the failed Egyptian campaign, Napoleon returned to what he knew best—beating up on other Europeans. He hiked over mountains, battled a league of countries that joined together to stop him, and never stopped winning. Whatever artworks he'd left behind the first time, he swept up in the second round. On the advice of Denon, Napoleon brought back a thousand items from German, Italian, and Spanish cities to put on display in his growing museum.

Napoleon liked his museum so much he got married there.

By the time of Napoleon's final defeat at Waterloo in 1815, the Louvre (which reverted to its original name after his defeat) was the biggest and best museum in the world. Visitors were overwhelmed by the displays, and more than a little impressed.

After Waterloo, Napoleon didn't care how impressed people were. He was in exile on the island of Elba, not allowed to conquer anything but the weeds taking over his garden. To him, the works of art he'd amassed were nothing more than war trophies, but to the rest of the world, it was the most incredible collection ever assembled in one place. The Louvre became a model for every other national art museum, and it *still* has one of the greatest collection of Old Masters along with Catherine the Great's Hermitage Museum in St. Petersburg (see Chapter 4).

Together, Napoleon and Denon achieved their goal of making Paris the art capital of the world. Artists came from all over to see, sketch, and be inspired by not only the "masters" but by art from places they never knew existed.

regions:

Turkey, modern-day Greece, North Africa, and the Middle East

Shortly after, a new style of art exploded on the scene that today is called *Orientalism*. Whether European artists traveled to these **regions**, or just looked at the pieces Napoleon brought back, they suddenly loved painting these "exotic" cultures, often in an over-stylized fashion that fit European stereotypes of the time. To them, that meant lots of palm trees, camels, and different styles of clothing.

It wasn't the only new artistic movement—Napoleon also brought back the classics with his Greek and Roman loot: pediments, marble statues, and Ionic columns. Europe, and America's founding fathers, were gaga for Greece. Art historians call it *Neoclassical*, which just means copying ancient Greece's classical styles.

Obviously, the countries Napoleon stole from were angry with him, and once he was defeated at Waterloo by the British, each of them made sure to ask for their stuff back in the peace treaty. The Louvre argued that they should keep the art because they'd taken better care of it with all those cleanings and restoration jobs, but nobody bought it.

The countries all got together at the Congress of Vienna to make a final decision. It was a heated debate around the world, but for the first time ever, the idea of returning booty was written into a legal treaty. Despite the treaty—and thanks to some smooth talking by Denon, claiming he "forgot" where he put items—the Louvre got to keep a little over half of their loot, enough to enable Paris keep the crown of the art capital of the Western world.

Not the columns!

Even so, over two thousand objects were returned. Crowds of weeping women surrounded the pieces to prevent their departure, but it didn't work. This was a new age, and even though Napoleon had stolen it all in the first place, the British victors of Waterloo decided not to plunder the Louvre for themselves as was normal. Instead, they gave the art to its previous owners, which was a pretty revolutionary move.

British artists were so impressed with the Louvre, they talked their government into starting its own painting gallery. Today, it's called the National Gallery. When the pope got his marbles back, he put them in a new location—what we call the Vatican Museum. During Napoleon's art-thirsty years, some cities even built museums as safe places to keep their art—examples include the Prado in Madrid and the Rijksmuseum in Amsterdam. And they all followed Denon's ideas on how to run a museum.

Mona Lisa:

See chapter 11 to read how she got to be so famous!

Napoleon had officially created the museum movement, even if he was only trying to glorify himself. But maybe he did appreciate art more than he let on. After all, he was the one who brought the forgotten **Mona Lisa** out of storage and hung her up in his bedroom when she was just a nobody.

You Decide: Should art in museums around the world be returned to the country that created it, even if the creators have been dead for hundreds of years?

Lived: 1775–1844, China
Occupation: Pirate Queen

Madame Cheng

No Parrots Needed

Anything You Can Do, I Can Do Better

Imagine a pirate. Does that pirate have facial hair, limited bathing habits, and walk with a peg-legged limp? Is the pirate a boy?

Don't worry, most of us probably picture bearded men with bad teeth and even worse accents sailing the high seas. But the most powerful pirate in the world had none of these things. Mostly because she was a woman from China.

In a time when women couldn't get jobs without catching a lot of side-eye, let alone become bosses, Cheng I Sao controlled the largest fleet of pirates the world has ever seen. Three world powers couldn't put a stop to her swashbuckling thievery. When she finally decided to quit the business, the golden age of piracy ended with her. She even got to keep her booty.

Cheng I Sao:

Her name translates literally as "Wife of Cheng."

She *was* the world's most interesting pirate.

A Sea Shanty Star Is Born

Cheng I Sao didn't start off powerful, but she did start off smart. In her time, the only way a woman could get ultimate power in China was to be a grandmother with lots of sons or to catch the eye of the emperor. But there was only one emperor, and a country full of women. Cheng I Sao decided she didn't need to be old, and she didn't need the emperor. Becoming a pirate would do.

She'd been born more common than dirt, but her future husband, Cheng I, didn't mind. And she didn't care that he'd be joining his family business, which included plundering, pillaging, and singing sea shanties on the open waters. In fact, she was delighted.

A born warrior bride.

A Chinese pirate's life was extremely different from that of a Western pirate. Chinese pirates welcomed women aboard—a practice that was often thought to be unlucky throughout the West. Whole families lived and fought together on ships on China's seas, usually crammed together in four-foot cabins to sleep at night. Women could wear whatever they wanted and beat up whomever annoyed them. They double-fisted cutlasses and defended their families living onboard. They would have scared the parrot right off of Black Blackbeard shoulder.

On Western ships, the crew members were more than likely there voluntarily, meaning they wanted to be swabbing poop off the decks while feeling the salt spray in their hair. If someone didn't want to be on a Chinese ship, it was probably because they were kidnapped and sold into ship-working slavery. The Chinese government estimated at the time that more than half of the pirate crew was there against their will. The practice made Chinese **fleets** much larger.

fleets:
At the height of Western piracy, there were 5,500 pirates. Under Madame Cheng, China had 70,000 pirates.

When Madame Cheng joined her new husband on board, it was business as usual: plunder **junks** and live off the loot, which included anything from valuables like silver and porcelain to food like rice, vegetables, sugar, and even fresh drinking water. When that wasn't enough, they stole from land-dwellers. Madame Cheng set about making her husband the most powerful pirate in the seas by corralling a bunch of other pirates under his command. It worked, and he became the head honcho of the area.

junks:
square Chinese ships with flat bottoms.

But then he died.

Madame Cheng wasn't typical, so it shouldn't be shocking that when a typhoon blew her husband overboard she didn't step down as co-leader and go into mourning, as a good Confucian wife should. She had more important things to do.

First on her list: become sole leader of all pirates. Second: world domination. Seriously.

Home sweet home aboard a Chinese junk.

To Live and Die

The early 1800s weren't prosperous times around the South China Sea for most residents. The ports of Canton and Macao had a lot of commerce thanks to ships sailing in and out, but taxes were high, competition for jobs was fierce, and the work didn't last all year long. Just because Confucius says it's better to starve than to steal doesn't mean regular people agreed. Lots of people were blurring the line of legal vs. illegal to survive. Pirating was like any other side job (if you weren't enslaved on the ship, of course). The Chengs and their **six squadrons** of pirates raided food and goods up and down the coast, stealing from poor villagers and rich men alike. Rice was rice no matter whose house it came from.

six squadrons:

Black, White, Yellow, Blue, Green, and Red Flag Squadrons. Madame Cheng sailed under the Red Flag Squadron.

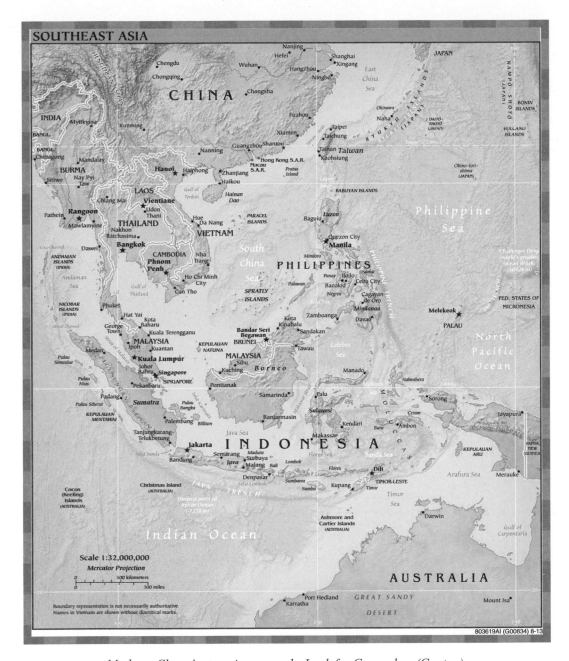

Madame Cheng's stomping grounds. Look for Guangzhou (Canton).

Once Cheng I died, it was a major task to keep the pirates together. Madame Cheng knew this, yet she also knew they were stronger together. United, they stood. On their own, the Chinese navy could pick off their ships one by one. Her smooth talking convinced all those pirates to not only stay together, but to also stay under her command. She made herself indispensable to the junk leaders, and she mined their loyalty like pirate gold.

Chang Pao:

As a good-looking young boy out fishing one day, Chang Pao was taken captive by Cheng I and adopted by the couple.

To solidify it all, she put her adopted son, **Chang Pao**, in charge of the largest squadron, the Red Flag Squadron, because everyone seemed to like him. Especially Madame Cheng. She liked him so much she made him her boyfriend soon after.

Don't let the name fool you. Chinese junks were ferociously fast.

With so many ships and pirates under her command (around four hundred junks and seventy thousand people), she needed a way to keep all those unruly men and women in line. She created a pirate's code, with her in charge of all commands and all punishments.

RULES:
- Ask Madame Cheng for the okay to attack.
- Give all plunder to the group fund.
- No pilfering from villagers or from the ships' group fund.
- Get permission before proposing to a lady.
- No cheating on your lady.
- No more hanging captives by their hair.
- No desertion.

Beheadings, lashings, quartering, and jailing were all common punishments, and Madame Cheng wasn't shy about using them. With her rules in place, she was ready to take on the world.

Fierce

Most Western pirates did a smash-and-grab heist. They'd target a vessel and try to scare the ship into surrendering by using their bloodred flags and dirty looks. If that didn't work, they'd disable the rigging, board the ship, kill the captain, and grab what they wanted. Captured ships were either sold or sunk.

This sort of practice wasn't going to feed seventy thousand hungry mouths, so, instead of sinking ships, Madame Cheng made them work for her. She forced vessels to pay for protection from pirates—which was her. It was like buying bully-protection from the bully.

The main vessels she liked to capture were ones carrying salt, and not because she liked her food well-seasoned. Salt was up there in importance with oxygen. Not only is salt essential to sustain life, but it helped keep food from spoiling before refrigeration was around. The tax on salt was the third most important source of money for the emperor.

How to Survive a Pirate Encounter

1. Give up your captain.
2. Hope someone will pay your ransom.
3. Stay on land.

Unfortunately for the emperor, only four of his 270 government salt ships were still his. The rest paid tribute to Madame Cheng. The going rate for protection was fifty Spanish silver dollars per one hundred **pao** of salt.

pao:

One pao equaled 293 pounds of salt.

It didn't take long for Madame Cheng to extend her operation from government salt ships to anything that floated. In order to sail her seas in peace, a ship had to buy a piece of paper signed by the pirates. It cost anywhere from fifty to five hundred silver coins for a one-way pass.

Most pirates like to stay mobile, but Madame Cheng didn't need to hide away on a deserted island or use Xs to mark the spot when she wanted to find her silver. Instead, she set up her agents in tax offices in main towns like Canton and Macao, right next door to the government tax offices.

Even simple fishermen bought protection passes and gave the pirates weapons while waving to officials. It didn't take long for some officials to see dollar signs and get in on the profit. Instead of stopping the pirates as they were ordered to do, they let Madame Cheng do what she wanted—for a hefty bribe. She would have anyway; this just made it easier.

Pretty soon, the emperor got sick of losing money. He wanted war against Madame Cheng and her pirates. His officials did not. Madame Cheng was scary. The emperor fired his governors and hired a bunch more. Then, he sent warships to the South China Sea. Madame Cheng defeated them all.

This bully means business.

Navy commanders began to stay onshore, claiming they were waiting for "favorable winds." When the emperor stopped buying their perpetual bad-weather story, they sabotaged their own ships to avoid her. Two commanders even committed suicide.

When Madame Cheng decided she needed more loot or food, she personally coordinated attacks. Chang Pao got so confident he'd post a notice in villages before swinging by and wait for the panic to set in. Then he'd take all their rice and money. If the villagers got the bright idea to fight back, Chang Pao burned the town to the ground, and let the pirates behead the villagers. Pirates aren't picky about who they kill.

With these sorts of tactics, it was only a matter of time before Madame Cheng took control of all the South China Sea. Her self-made economy in the area wielded far more power than any emperor's. China's trade almost ceased with all foreign powers.

Due to the long distance, British and Portuguese traders only came once a year, and they didn't want to lose their source of profitable Chinese goodies because of one out-of-control woman. The emperor didn't want to stop selling Chinese silk and tea to the West, either. Madame Cheng was putting a wrinkle in everyone's silk robes.

China in the early nineteenth century wanted Western assistance about as much as they wanted smallpox. So when the emperor finally decided to ask for help in changing Madame Cheng's tide, it meant he seriously needed the help. He asked the "barbarians" (British and Portuguese ships with some American volunteers) to go in with cannons blazing and exterminate the pirates.

It didn't work.

Instead of making the pirates fall in line, the Westerners were forced to negotiate with Chang Pao in order to stay alive. Madame Cheng was closer to world domination than an evil genius stroking a fluffy white cat.

The emperor debating the lesser of two evils; barbarians it is.

Their Own Worst Enemy

Finally, the emperor caught a break. The pirates turned on one another. Some were jealous that Chang Pao was Madame Cheng's boyfriend. They thought she should be dating them instead. Others wanted to quit while they were ahead. Since the emperor couldn't beat them, he decided to have them join him. He was so desperate to stop Madame Cheng that he offered her pirates pardons and cushy government jobs.

With everything on their side, you'd think the pirates would refuse. They didn't. Fleets formally under Madame Cheng's protection swallowed the dangling carrot, and used the stick to beat their way out of Madame Cheng's fleet.

amnesty:
an official way to say, "You're forgiven. Now stop stealing already!"

The Black Flag Squadron surrendered their junks first in exchange for **amnesty**, giving the other pirates something to chew on. In three weeks, nine thousand more pirates joined the traitors, taking many of Madame Cheng's cannons with them.

Madame Cheng hadn't come this far only to lose everything, and neither had Chang Pao, who vowed to keep fighting. A few days later, they defeated more Chinese and Portuguese ships. Finally, the two outlaws decided they could still be rich without being fugitives.

Chang Pao went to the negotiating table first. When the officials told him he'd have to hand over his junks and live on land like some earth slug, he didn't take it well. He was a born seaman; he was ready to stop being a pirate, but not to stop sailing. Negotiations ground to a halt.

Madame Cheng would have to take matters into her own hands. As usual.

Stubborn as a Mule

Madame Cheng knew how to show someone she meant business. She walked into the port at Canton unarmed with a bunch of women as her escort. She was pretty confident—after all, she had a whole fleet of ships with their guns aimed at port. If terms couldn't be reached, she'd go right back to being a huge pain in the butt.

She didn't waver from Chang Pao's terms, and somehow, the governor gave in. Chang Pao got to keep twenty to thirty junks for his own salt-trade business, a rank in the army, a salary, and his life. She arranged for a **bunch of her men** to go straight and join the army if they wished, too. Maybe because the emperor knew she would do it anyway, she was also allowed to keep her loot. Madame Cheng officially received the best retirement package in the history of piracy after less than three years on the job.

This was no celebrity situation, where she might retire, and then stage a comeback a few years later, bigger and better than ever. Her retirement was for good, and in her wake, she left junk-sized shoes to fill. Nobody was up to the task. The largest pirate confederacy the world has ever seen collapsed with the lowering of her sails.

Obviously, Madame Cheng suddenly found herself with a lot of time on her hands. Nothing would be as exciting as ordering thousands of swashbuckling pirates into battle, and gardening was so cliché.

First, she decided to make an honest man out of Chang Pao. They got married, and he went off to fight against his once-fellow pirates. Next, Madame Cheng opened a gambling den. Instead of gambling on her own life, she now let others bet theirs away. She always did have a good head for business.

Madame Cheng died at the pretty old age of sixty-nine, the exact opposite of a good Confucian wife till the end. The emperor and his heir, on the other hand, did not learn their lesson about messing with pirates. Instead of realizing their weaknesses and beefing up their navy, they considered themselves invincible and their control of the South China Sea restored.

It **wasn't**.

bunch of her men:

But not all! Instead of amnesty, 350 of her men got a swift kick out of China's doors into exile. An unlucky 126 of them were beheaded.

wasn't:

Check out chapter 7, "Robert Fortune," to watch the First and Second Opium Wars unfold.

It's Not a Pirate's Life for Me

English sailor Richard Glasspoole made the mistake of assuming the large fleet of ships he saw in the South China Sea distance were simply fishing boats. They were actually fishing for victims, and Glasspoole soon found himself on the hook of Madame Cheng's pirates. For the next eleven weeks, Glasspoole helped show the Chinese pirates how to use Western guns in exchange for keeping his head. Like any self-respecting prisoner, he also kept a diary of his experiences.

These included watching the pirates drink wine mixed with gunpowder for "courage," cook the hearts of their enemies to eat with rice (more "courage"), and lots of card-playing. He claims to have also been sprinkled with garlic water to gain protection from bullets, and to have eaten caterpillars along with the pirates when food become scarce. Glasspoole eventually got lucky—he was ransomed for 7,654 Spanish silver dollars and went off to publish his diary.

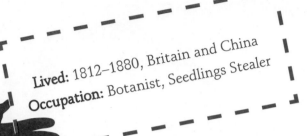

Lived: 1812–1880, Britain and China
Occupation: Botanist, Seedlings Stealer

Chapter 7

Robert Fortune

The Gardener Spy

For the Love of Tea!

Robert Fortune was no James Bond. In fact, he was pretty much the opposite of 007. He was a gardener from Scotland. The only thing he had in common with Bond was his boss; they both worked for Britain.

Thanks to the slightly excessive British love of tea and crumpets, the gardener Robert Fortune found himself sneaking around China in the 1840s disguised as a **mandarin** for the ultimate double-cross. His mission? Steal tea seeds.

Even though he (and his mission) didn't seem flashy, Fortune had an explosive impact on the world. He expanded one empire and decimated another. Countries gained whole new economies thanks to his theft. All for the love of tea.

> **mandarin:**
> A Chinese public official. Mandarins worked for the government during the age of imperial dynasties.

Green Hands

Robert Fortune thought dirt was the coolest; it grew plants! He'd play in the dirt all day long if only someone would pay him for it. The only problem with making his hobby his full-time job was his social situation. He was no gentleman—at least, not by British standards in the Victorian era (1837–1901).

Fortune probably still opened doors for ladies and bowed to the queen, but he had to work for a living. Victorian "gentlemen" had enough family money they never needed to work. They could garden all day! For fun!

Because of Fortune's no-money thing, gentleman gardeners didn't want him in their "I heart **bleeding hearts**" clubs, like the Royal Horticultural Society. If Fortune wanted an invite, he had to start at the bottom and work his way up the ivy-covered ladder of acceptance.

Thanks to Fortune's green thumb, fingers, and hands, he raced up it. He could charm even the most finicky flowers into blooming, like delicate orchids and temperamental ornamentals. No one was better at flower-whispering, so for an important plant mission into mysterious China, Fortune was the Royal Horticultural Society's first choice.

Wait for me!

bleeding hearts:

These flowers have petals in the shape of dripping hearts, and they were actually discovered by Fortune on his first trip to China in 1845. But that didn't mean he could join the club.

China was one large question mark on Westerners' maps. The West was so confused about the large mass of land, they just drew scary pictures of monsters in that general direction and wrote, "Here be dragons." That's because China had kept its doors closed to foreigners for centuries, except for the coastal trading port in Canton. British traders only came once a year, had to stay on their boats, and had to pay in cold, hard silver for Chinese goods, including tea, porcelain, and silks.

That all changed thanks to a war over flowers.

Flower power. (Poppy left, tea right.)

Opium War Number One

The first flower is the *Camellia sinensis*. (You can just call it tea.) Besides being beautiful, the caffeine from brewed tea is a mild stimulant, and it provided workers with the get-up-and-go energy that industrial Britain needed to crank out new technology like the steam engine and the cotton gin. Tea also required boiled water, meaning all those nasty buggers lurking in unclean water were killed. That made dysentery, typhoid, and cholera a thing of pre-tea days. Even cold tea has antiseptic qualities that stopped deadly bacteria from growing. That's not to mention how tasty it was, especially with some milk and sugar for extra calories. The British were addicted.

The only place to get the tea Britain craved, however, was China. This meant China had a global monopoly. Unfortunately for the Brits, China still had a strict silver-only policy, and silver was something the British were running low on after a war with the American colonies cut off their silver supply from the New World. Their one-sided trading partnership with China was costing Britain's Queen Victoria way too much money! Luckily for her, she knew of a second flower.

Papaver somniferum comes from a poppy seed. It sounds innocent, but poppies aren't just grown for their seeds to top bagels. Some species are harvested for other uses—illegal ones. A certain type of poppy produces a thick white substance that is used to make opium, a highly addictive drug that historically was used for medicinal purposes and can still be found today in medicines such as morphine.

The powerful **East India Trading Company** harvested the poppy in India and sold the manufactured, potent form of the drug in China on behalf of Queen Victoria for pure silver. Secretly—of course—because officially the Chinese emperor outlawed opium. That didn't stop the addicted from buying it anyway. Now, Victoria could have her tea and sip it, too.

The Chinese emperor had a big problem on his hands. His people became seriously addicted to opium, and his silver was flowing the wrong way, bankrupting the Chinese government.

East India Trading Company:

This was a royally approved company that traveled east to places like India and Southeast Asia for goods only grown and produced there. It was a powerhouse in the world market and deeply involved in politics to increase British influence.

In 1839, the Chinese did something drastic to stop the flow of opium. They confiscated and destroyed over a year's worth of British opium. And just so the queen knew they meant business, they also took British opium merchants as hostages. Queen Victoria couldn't take that sitting down, so she sent her navy to fight the First Opium War.

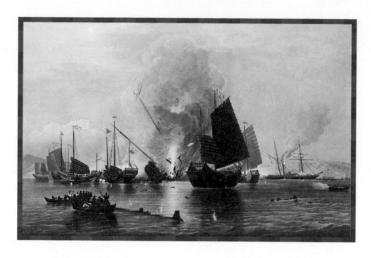

The British iron-boat Nemesis shooting wooden Chinese junks like fish in a barrel.

chance:

Although the emperor thought he did, because of his dad's "victory" against Madame Cheng's pirates (See chapter 6). He had no idea about his navy's weaknesses, because they hadn't been truly tested against the pirates—the pirates had just been bought off.

Against the technological superiority of the British navy, the wooden Chinese junks (boats) didn't stand a chance. China may have invented gunpowder, but Britain took it to another level by arming their steam-powered, metal warships with heavy artillery. By 1842, Britain forced China to give Hong Kong to them, to pay for the ruined opium, and to open five of their ports to trading instead of one. In return, Queen Victoria gave up . . . nothing.

Top Hat Not Necessary

Queen Victoria forced open China's door a crack with the Treaty of Nanking, allowing Robert Fortune to sneak through for his high society bosses.

Because Fortune wasn't a gentleman, the Royal Horticulturalist Society figured the mere prestige of going on this trip should be enough for him. They didn't want to give him a salary, weapons, or support, but he talked them into giving him a rifle for protection since he argued the mission would be a failure if he died. The Society grudgingly agreed. They ponied up a slim salary, too. He was the first Westerner granted permission by the British to travel to China after the war.

For three years, Fortune trekked mostly around the coast, taking notes and collecting anything that looked cool to him. Thanks to the newly opened ports, he "discovered" armloads of fruits and flowers for the Royal Horticulturalist Society. When he got home, he published his diary and became a mega hit. The snooty societies were glad to have him in their clubs now!

To the amazed British, Fortune was now an expert in everything Asian. So when the rich East India Trading Company came calling with a bigger and better traveling opportunity, Fortune listened.

They wanted him back in China, this time for tea seeds. The British had decided on one thing: they couldn't rely on smuggling opium and getting silver to pay for their tea anymore. In order to have an endless supply for their endless thirst, they needed to control the growing of tea plants themselves.

A Hairier Fairy Godmother

Newly forced-open China was a dangerous place for foreigners, and Robert Fortune stuck out like a neon highlighter. For one, he was freakishly tall for his time. Hovering a foot over most men made it hard to blend in. His Scottish blood and disturbingly long nose didn't help matters either. During his travels, he was more likely to get punched in the face than find someone willing to share the ancient secrets of tea-making. That's why his first order of business in China was to hire two all-purpose men. They'd be his guides, etiquette enforcers, and bodyguards.

Fortune's new best friends could look past the height and nose thing—for the right price. They gave him one condition: Fortune had to look the part. Getting caught hundreds of miles away from the trading ports would mean death for all of them.

Like two grumpy fairy godmothers, they pulled a Cinderella. First, they turned Fortune's European hair into a passable braided Manchu queue, which took a lot of elbow grease and razor blades. Next, they shoved him into a silk robe and stuffed his giant feet into thin slippers. Along with his extreme makeover, he needed a new name. He changed it to Sing-Wa, which means Bright Flower.

If anyone got suspicious about his accent, height, or lack of comprehension, Fortune would sit back and let his servants imply that his speech was "court dialect" or that he was a mandarin from across the Great Wall. Everyone knew the emperor's subjects on that side of the Wall were brutish and tall.

Fortune and his friends' first destination was a steamship-hop away in the green-tea district. One of Fortune's hired men, Wang, finagled his way into a green-tea factory. All Fortune had to do was keep quiet and take notes. The workers showed him how to dry the leaves in the sun for an hour before stir-frying them in a huge wok. He watched the leaves crunch under bamboo rollers on long tables until they were a fraction of their original size, before they were packed up for shipping.

Just a little off the top, please.

Fortune was stealing China's ancient history right from under their noses.

Next, Fortune went to Wang's family home at the foot of Sung-Lo Mountain and gathered all the tea seeds he could find. The first Westerner to venture into tea land, Fortune only needed a week to collect thousands of green-tea seeds. A few more trips to other green-tea regions brought his grand total up to ten thousand tea seeds and thirteen thousand **seedlings**.

Usually his eyes were a lot bigger than his hands and he'd have to store all the seeds on the chair his hired men were supposed to be carrying him in. But it was worth it. Soon he was ready to ship his stolen treasures off to British-controlled India.

Spoiled

For the longest time, people weren't sure if green tea and black tea were separate plants. Frankly, no one knew what the tealeaf was going on in China. On his first trip, Fortune found out that both green and black tea came from the same plant, but that the best green tea grew in lower hills and the best black tea in higher mountains. The real differences, however, came from the production. (Literal) spoiler alert: black tea is left out in the sun to rot for a day, which is how it turns black.

seedlings: tiny, young plants grown from seeds.

Imagine climbing those hills to work every day.

It takes six years for a tea seed to grow into a productive tea plant, so Fortune treated his seedlings like babies, tucking them into soil and singing them lullabies as he closed their Wardian Cases. As for the seeds, Fortune crossed his fingers and layered them into bags with burnt rice on the advice of an old Chinese gardener. Fortune was getting pretty good at the covert spy thing.

Little did he know that all of his careful packaging was for nothing.

When at First You Don't Succeed

Fortune spent the next three months combing the prettier-than-a-postcard Wuyi Mountains for black tea seeds. His green tea seeds had ended up with the East India Company's gardeners in Calcutta, India, but that didn't mean they were safe. The whole point of a Wardian Case is to *not* open it. Instead, an overexcited government official couldn't wait to see what was going on inside, and that's all it took to kill nearly all of the tea seeds and seedlings before they could reach their final destination: the Himalaya Mountains. So

What's in a Wardian Case?

As you can imagine, keeping plants alive during a long sea voyage in the nineteenth century posed quite a challenge. Fresh water was in low supply during long voyages, and no self-respecting sailor would choose a plant over himself for watering. The plants also needed sunlight to grow, but this exposed them to the damaging saltwater spray. The problem seemed impossible, until Dr. Nathaniel Bagshaw Ward solved it—by accident.

Around 1829, Dr. Ward was experimenting with moth cocoons in closed bottles when a fern spore popped up out of the blue. He left the bottle alone for four years (no word on the fate of the moths) and kept notes as the fern grew. He tried other plants and birds, and lo and behold, they all thrived in bottles without regular watering. Except for the birds. They didn't make it.

Plants can survive for years if left alone in a sealed, sunlight-infused environment. The soil in the glass provided moisture, while the sun provided food via photosynthesis. Wardian Cases are still used today for decorative purposes. They're just called terrariums now.

So that's what's in a Wardian Case . . .

far, Fortune's success rate was at three percent. You can't crush an empire with a rate like that.

Over in China, Fortune continued his hunt with his bodyguards in tow. Like a crime-scene detective, he took meticulous notes, except in this case, he was the one committing the crimes. He needed to know everything if the next seeds he stole were going to survive, including the right soil, water, altitude, and care of the tea plants.

To gather more black-tea seeds, he gave street "urchins" a few coins to grab as many as they could find and layered the seeds into his Wardian Cases. By then, he'd heard about the deaths of his babies and decided to store all the seeds in the glass boxes with strict Do Not Open instructions. He sent another thirteen thousand seeds to his bosses in India and crossed his fingers and toes that the shipment would survive this time. After three years undercover, Fortune's job was done.

Tea and Opium Go Together like Peanut Butter and Jelly

treachery:

including being lied to, internal bickering, gambling behind his back, and eventually being completely deserted by all but one of his hired chair-carriers.

Robert Fortune had traveled up and down mountains, survived **treachery** by his hired men, and crossed monsoon-swollen rivers, all to obtain viable tea seedlings. And they were thriving. Now he needed to convince Chinese tea experts to betray their emperor and their country by coming with him to India.

Rumors of man-eating tigers in malaria-infested jungles made the trip sort of a hard sell, but Fortune managed to find eight tea experts willing to leave their families behind for a paycheck. Two died soon after reaching India, and the rest hated their new life, but Fortune had fulfilled his duty. Along with the experts, Fortune shipped all sorts of tea-making tools, including huge woks and spatulas, to India. Eventually he also made the journey to check on their progress.

The Himalayas were so perfect for tea that even the measly three percent of green tea seedlings that had survived were thriving by the time Fortune arrived. He could return home satisfied.

Darjeeling, India:

Tea from Darjeeling is the Ferrari of black teas. People pay out the nose to smell its floral nose (aroma).

By the 1880s, Britain had cut the market for tea out from under China, and by the turn of the century, the Chinese exported less than ten percent of the world's tea. Fortune's babies in India were all grown up and British-occupied India was now the number one exporter of tea in the world. All of the black tea produced in Darjeeling, India, came from Fortune's original stolen seeds.

China took the loss of their tea market pretty hard. They called their next period the Century of

Humiliation. It wasn't just the loss of their tea trade; rebellions and revolutions ruled the land, and some say the humiliation didn't end until Britain gave Hong Kong back in 1997. The loss of their monopoly on tea, which had been their most valuable export, destroyed China's economy, and they still had to deal with the widespread problem of opium addiction. By the beginning of the twentieth century, China was consuming 85–95 percent of all the opium in the world. No wonder the Chinese didn't want the British there in the first place.

Tea became cheap and easily accessible worldwide. It was the first mass-marketed and mass-produced product. Everyone but the tea-dumping Americans drank it.

So the next time you're offered a teacup, don't roll your eyes. Sit back, sip your brew to the dregs, and remember: people have done grisly things for all the tea in China.

Lived: 1839–1915, America
Occupation: Steamboat Captain, Congressman

Robert Smalls

Motoring

read:

By South Carolina law, slaves couldn't be educated, but Smalls didn't always follow the law. During the war, he hired a tutor and told a reporter, "I stole it in the night, Sir."

Civil War:

After years of arguing over slavery, a few Southern states, led by South Carolina, called themselves the Confederate States of America and left the United States of America (the Union) after President Abraham Lincoln was elected. This was because Lincoln opposed the spread of slavery. Four years of bloody war followed. Eventually, the Confederacy lost and rejoined the Union.

Not Your Average Thief

Robert Smalls couldn't **read** or write, but he knew other important things, like how to steer a boat and where to avoid Confederate underwater mines. Probably because he's the one that put them in the water in the first place.

Smalls knew the Union army would also like to know these things, so he stole a boat and sailed around all those explosives to get to his new friends. Typically, boat thieves aren't heroes, but Robert Smalls wasn't typical. He was a slave during the **Civil War**, stuck with the Confederates in Charleston, South Carolina. He hated being a slave, so he decided to change his destiny by sailing to freedom. His theft not only set him free, it made him a hero to many—and it changed history.

Taking Control

Robert Smalls grew up a slave on the McKee plantation in Beaufort, South Carolina. Scholars say the McKees treated Robert relatively better than their other slaves. It might have had something to do with the fact that his master, John McKee, was *possibly* his father. People didn't talk about it, but Robert grew up playing with his half-brother, Henry McKee, and even sleeping in the same room, just like regular brothers. Unlike regular brothers, Robert slept on the floor in order to get Henry anything he needed in the middle of the night.

It got even more uncomfortable. When John McKee died, Robert and his mother passed into the hands of Henry. Now, Robert's half-brother owned him. Henry was nicer to Robert than he was to his other slaves. Whenever Robert broke curfew, he knew Henry would bail him out of jail.

curfew:
Slaves had to obey a curfew. They couldn't be out past ten p.m. without their masters or a written note from them.

Because of this illusion of freedom, Robert's mother was worried he was too comfortable with his life. She wanted him to know what slavery truly meant for millions of the enslaved and to prepare him for whatever his future might be in case he was ever sold. So she took him into town to watch slave auctions and beatings. Her methods were effective. Robert craved real freedom.

Luckily, Robert was a pretty good negotiator. He talked Henry into letting him leave home in a process called hiring out. Robert could make a little bit of money doing odd jobs as long as he paid Henry fifteen dollars a month from his wages.

Robert left Beaufort when he was only twelve years old and moved to Charleston. In order to make sure everyone in sight knew he was a still a slave, he had to wear a metal badge that said the year and the job he was hired to do. It was demeaning, but at least he was making money.

A slave badge was a constant reminder that someone owned you.

stevedore:

a person who unloads and loads ships.

Robert built a life in Charleston, waiting on tables, lighting lamps, and unloading ships. Eventually, he worked his way up from **stevedore** to ship rigger to sailor. He needed all the extra money he could make, because he was still determined to buy his freedom.

In his spare time, Robert met a woman he liked. Hannah Jones was a slave, too, which meant he'd have to buy her freedom as well.

Hannah worked as a hotel maid, and her owner demanded eight hundred dollars for the freedom of her and the couple's infant daughter. Robert was getting paid sixteen dollars a month as a deckhand; at that rate, it would take eight hundred months before he could buy his family's freedom! Even though

Smalls still found time for love in his balancing act.

Hannah took in sailors' laundry and Robert moonlighted as a stevedore for extra cash, it would still take a lifetime. There was always the chance that Hannah's owner would sell her and their daughter, too. If that happened, Smalls could come home from work to an empty home—and he wouldn't be able to do anything about it.

At the beginning of the Civil War, Robert found work on a cotton-hauling ship turned Confederate warship called the *Planter*. The white captain made Smalls head pilot, but since he was a slave, they just called him a wheelman.

Smalls navigated the tricky harbor—which was full of hidden reefs, sand-bars, and treacherous water currents—for the Confederate army. Instead of hauling cotton, now the *Planter* hauled guns, ammunition, and soldiers to the various forts in Charleston. With a pivot gun and a Howitzer (see picture), it destroyed Union lighthouses and planted underwater mines. According to newspapers of the time, the *Planter* was the most valuable ship in the harbor. Smalls had big plans for it.

The Planter decked out for war.

Thanks to his white father, his skin was a bit lighter than the rest of the slaves on the ship. In the right light, and wearing the captain's can't-miss-it straw hat, Robert could even pass for the white captain. The slaves on board joked about stealing the ship, but Robert was dead serious about the plan. He had to be serious, or he'd just be dead for even joking about it. Even more important, Hannah had recently given birth to their son. The cost of his family's freedom was skyrocketing.

When Smalls put out feelers among the other enslaved crew members to see how they felt about becoming free, he found that most of them felt pretty good about it. Even if they had to steal it. Even if they had to die for it.

Freedom or Bust

Robert Smalls formed a plan of escape, and it was way better than running like heck for the Mason-Dixon Line. All afternoon on May 12, 1862, stevedores loaded artillery and guns onto the *Planter* to carry to nearby forts. Smalls deliberately slowed the workers down, forcing the ship to stay in harbor for another night. The captain didn't mind the extra time in town. He and the rest of the white crew stayed on land for some unauthorized time off,

A 24-pounder Howitzer, not locked and loaded.

leaving Smalls in charge. Exactly what they weren't supposed to do.

Smalls got word to all the enslaved crew members' wives and kids, including his own, that it was time. Everything about the plan was risky. The captain had wanted to leave early the next morning with the tide, so he could return at any moment to prepare. Robert had to get the loud engines up and running at around three a.m. and keep his fingers crossed that no Confederate soldiers guarding the harbor entrance would think it strange for the ship to be departing at that time.

Then, Smalls broke into the captain's quarters, slipped into the captain's uniform, and put on that straw hat. Keeping casual was the key, although the early morning darkness and steam from the ship would help. Robert had been miming the captain's poses all day in order to look more authentic. Now he had to get through five forts chock-full of heavy artillery before he could get to open water and freedom ten miles away.

Robert knew where all the hidden mines in the harbor were, and he knew the currents and high sandbars that could wreck the *Planter*. He safely guided the boat through these dangers and into the line of fire of Fort Sumter's massive defensives. It took a cool head to look a gun in the muzzle and keep going, but he had to—the whole crew would be shot if they were caught.

When he came upon a checkpoint, Smalls used the right code whistles (kind of like knowing the knocks to gain entry to a secret clubhouse meeting) and kept chugging toward open water. In case someone decided to take a closer look, Robert flipped the collar of the captain's uniform up, pulled down that straw hat, and shouted hello, just as the captain normally would. It was 4:15 a.m. by the time they got to Fort Sumter, and they still had seven miles to go. If anyone got suspicious at the fort, they'd be planted in the bottom of the water, feeding the fish.

As soon as he got past the massive guns at Fort Sumter, Smalls gunned the *Planter* like a race car, only two hundred miles per hour slower, and headed straight to the nearest Union ship—the USS *Onward*—to wave a white bedsheet of surrender.

At first, the Union commanders thought they were under attack, perhaps by one crazed Confederate. They prepared to fire on the *Planter* until they saw a white flag of surrender. Smalls saluted while the rest of his crew started cheering and waving. The *Onward* got the idea quickly, and welcomed the

Don't make any sudden movements . . .

sixteen men, women, and children to freedom. The four cannons, two hundred rounds of ammunition, and the boat itself were the icing on the cake.

Even better, Robert had managed to bring the Confederate's navy codebook. With a grin, he handed it over to the Union commander. Now the Union knew all the secret handshakes to get into the clubhouse, too. It was exactly the type of information that would lead the Union to victory.

The Union navy commander called Robert's leadership "one of the coolest and most gallant naval acts of war." Then he offered him and his crew $4,500 in reward money to share among them.

Across the water, the Confederates didn't find it as cool. According to their version of events, it was "one of the most shameful events of this or any other war." Confederate officers said the white crew of the *Planter* should be thrown out of the army and put in either **petticoats** or straightjackets. They put the white crew on trial. Some still didn't believe a black man could have masterminded the theft. They insisted, "Some white must be at the bottom of it." Really, they should have given due credit to Smalls.

petticoats: garments women wore under dresses. Not only did white men of the nineteenth century think black men didn't have the courage to fight, they didn't think women did, either.

After his daring escape, Smalls could've decided to enjoy freedom the safe way—out of uniform. But he didn't. Staying idle wasn't his style, and he laughed at the two-thousand-dollar reward the Confederates put on his head. At a time when black men weren't welcomed, even in the Union army, he stayed on with the Union navy as a pilot, anyway, and helped remove the same mines he'd laid for the Confederates. He kept sailing the stolen *Planter* into battle, too, even though he still wasn't called captain. Seventeen battles, to be exact.

Once, the *Planter* came under heavy fire from Confederates, so its white captain ordered Robert to beach the *Planter* and put their hands over their heads. Surrendering was fine for the white guys, but Robert decided there was no way he'd let himself be taken back into slavery.

While the captain cowered in the cabin below, Robert took command of the ship and sailed through bullets to freedom, again. When they reached safety, the Union commander dismissed the cowardly captain and promoted Robert. He was the first black captain in U.S. history. Now he made $150 a month, and none of it had to go to his half-brother Henry.

Playing the Publicity Game

Robert was smart about his victory. He knew the value of celebrity before there were people like publicists and agents telling him how to self-promote. He kept his story alive by taking pictures aboard the Planter and giving interviews.

It was an instant success. National magazines and newspapers raved about him, and the military named a fort after him.

Even President Lincoln couldn't wait to meet this man.

Only three months after his theft, Robert Smalls found himself in front of Lincoln and his secretary of war, Edwin Stanton. At this time, no one was sure what to do about slaves. Could they fight? Would they want to fight?

Smalls administered a big dose of truth. Black men not only had intelligence, they had heart and bravery. They could and they would fight; Lincoln just needed to wake up and smell the facts.

Of course, it seems silly to think black men didn't have the guts for gore and glory, but many people didn't believe it back then. Smalls set the record straight and insisted on allowing black men to fight for their freedom. It worked, and he carried home a direct order from Secretary Stanton to enlist five thousand slaves in the Union army and to set them and their families free. Robert balanced his job as captain with various speaking tours, where he encouraged men to enlist. By the end of the war, over two hundred thousand black recruits served the Union cause.

The 4th U.S. Colored Infantry ready to make history.

For Beaufort

Suddenly, Smalls was famous, and he used that fame to become a politician and to help black people in the uncertain times after the war. The rules of life had changed now that slavery was **abolished**, and Smalls was just the guy to help up write a set of new ones.

abolished:
Congress passed the Thirteenth Amendment outlawing slavery and "involuntary servitude" (except as a criminal punishment) on December 6, 1865.

Instead of getting free meals or skipping long grocery store lines, Smalls used his celebrity to raise funds and food for recently freed slaves to help them transition into their new lives. He founded a school and bought a house. With forty other people, he helped organize the first Republican Party in South Carolina, which was the party of President Lincoln in the nineteenth century.

When he ran for the South Carolina House of Representatives and, later, the South Carolina Senate, everyone knew he'd sweep the elections. Smalls used his street smarts and his *Planter* story to build up a political machine in his home town of Beaufort. He couldn't lose if he tried. In fact, he didn't lose until **Reconstruction** ended. When Federal troops left the South, it allowed white Democrats to take control of elections by intimidation and bullying.

Reconstruction:
The period following the Civil War that aimed to help the Southern states get back into the Union and transition former slaves into a life of freedom. The federal government sent Union troops to the South to force the Southern states comply, but after Hayes was elected president in 1877, he ordered them to leave.

Before Rosa Parks

Streetcars were popular in the 1860s. They were like buses today, except noisier, dirtier, and slower, but they beat walking. In December 1864, Smalls was in Philadelphia waiting for the *Planter* to be repaired. He bided his time with speaking engagements and learning how to read. When it began to rain, Smalls and a white sailor decided to ride back to the shipyard by streetcar.

The conductor refused to let Smalls sit, because rail companies could decide whether black people could ride their streetcars, even in free states. If Smalls wanted a ride, he'd have to stand in the rain on the platform. (Eleven of the nineteen companies in Philadelphia refused service to black people and the other eight made them stand on the un-shaded platform.) His sailor friend tried to explain who Smalls was, but it didn't matter. The conductor wasn't budging.

They decided to walk instead. There was some uproar over the Civil War hero's treatment and even a boycott of the streetcars. Despite all the protesting, however, only a few of the rail companies gave in and banned discrimination. It wasn't until 1867—after more sit-ins and demonstrations—that a law was passed integrating streetcars, which allowed people of all races to ride together. It didn't last long. By 1904, legal segregation was back thanks to Jim Crow laws, and once again, Smalls was asked to give up his seat on a streetcar. Again, he decided he'd rather walk. It would take the courage of Rosa Parks and other civil rights activists in the 1960s before discrimination on public transportation would be made illegal again.

Smalls didn't bow out of politics after one little defeat. He won the next hotly contested election and used his seat in Congress to get a post office for Beaufort.

Altogether, he served five terms in the House of Representatives in Washington. Smalls hadn't been able to go to school, so he spent a lot of his time in office trying to get free education to kids everywhere. He never stopped believing that, given equal opportunities, black people could perform equally in anything.

men:

Women of any race couldn't vote until the Nineteenth Amendment was ratified in 1920.

In 1868, Smalls helped draft a new state constitution that granted equal rights to black and white **men**, but discrimination still ruled the day. It would get worse once Reconstruction ended in 1877.

Apparently unable to make up their minds, South Carolina drafted another state constitution in 1895. It essentially took away African Americans' right to vote. Robert Smalls was the only representative brave enough to stand up and say that it was wrong. He was also the only one to vote against it. The constitution set the stage for Jim Crow laws to be passed. These laws created separate and unequal everything, despite their official "separate but equal" slogan.

On a scale of 1 to 10, how distinguished do I look?

Smalls tried to fight against this growing movement to take away his rights, yet again, but by his death in 1915, Jim Crow laws were in full force. It wouldn't be until Congress passed the Civil Rights Act in 1964, ending legal segregation, that Smalls's dream would begin to be realized. However, one court decision didn't change everyone's mind suddenly, and equality is *still* a battle being fought today.

For fifty years, Robert Smalls was the most powerful black man in South Carolina, and he always used his position to look out for Beaufort, which made him a local legend, although a national legend would have fit the bill, too. His thieving helped people, including President Abraham Lincoln, see the truth: black people deserved freedom, and they were brave enough to take it.

Celebrity Cribs: Smalls Edition

With all the money Robert Smalls's celebrity status earned him, he decided to splurge. He snapped up buildings, houses, and town lots all over his old town of Beaufort. In 1863, he bought the plantation where he'd grown up, the McKee house on Prince Street. Smalls even invited old Mrs. McKee to live there when he learned of her money troubles, and she accepted. Smalls didn't stop there. When the McKee family asked for financial help, he sent money and pulled strings to get one member into the Naval Academy.

"Separate Is Not Equal"

In the century between the Civil War and the 1960s, over four hundred laws were passed that made segregation legal. These Jim Crow laws were meant to humiliate anyone who wasn't white. From telephone booths to railcars to schools and restaurants, African Americans couldn't use the same (nicer) facilities that white people used. It wasn't just separate toilets. States made it illegal to marry anyone of a different race, or have children with them. In South Carolina, black people couldn't adopt a white child.

Other states made playing games together, like baseball or checkers, against the law. Even convicted white criminals had more rights—it was illegal to chain together a white man and a black man. States continue to wrangle with the legacy of Jim Crow laws to this day.

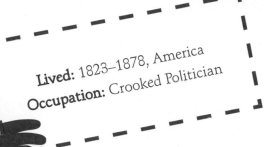

Chapter 9

Lived: 1823–1878, America
Occupation: Crooked Politician

William Tweed

The Boss

Big Tastes

Everything about Boss Tweed was big. From his waistband to his bank account to his ten-karat diamond bling, the Boss lived large. Literally. He topped the scales at three hundred pounds, something his archnemesis **Thomas Nast** never let him forget.

Nast isn't short for nasty, but he acted that way toward the Boss. He drew cartoons for *Harper's Weekly* magazine depicting the Boss in not very nice ways. Maybe because Boss Tweed was more crooked than a broken finger, and Nast wanted to the world to see that.

Thomas Nast:

The cartoonist was also responsible for the modern imagery of Santa Claus as well as the Republican Party's elephant and the Democratic Party's donkey.

THE "BRAINS"
That achieved the Tammany Victory at the Rochester Democratic Convention.

The original Mr. Moneybags: A Thomas Nast interpretation

Thomas Nast's cartoons helped bring down the thief who stole millions from New York City. But the Boss's story is way more complicated than good guys and bad guys. This Robin Hood stole from the rich to give to himself, his friends, *and* to the poor. The Boss's downfall had rippling effects throughout New York City, kind of like throwing a gigantic boulder into a lake.

This is the story of Boss Tweed: The big-hearted big thief.

Breaking the Law Never Looked So Easy

Boss Tweed started out life as Bill Tweed, local fireman. If your apartment building caught on fire in 1850s New York, you crossed your fingers and hoped a volunteer crew stopped by in time. There were no fire hydrants, just volunteers hand-pumping water. By the time of Tweed, volunteer departments fought each other to get to a fire first, because it meant political support from the people they saved and the honor of being heroic.

alderman:

an elected member of the city government who helps the residents in their district, called a ward. Think of aldermen like little neighborhood mayors with lots of power.

Tweed liked to lead the charge at these brawls, and he was really good at punching someone's lights out while buildings burned to a crisp. His friends voted him foreman, and he used his popularity to win the first election he ran in: **alderman** of the seventh ward.

This first political position propelled him to national politics in Washington, D.C., where he sat in the House of Representatives.

Tweed found life there pretty dull compared to the hustle and bustle of his New York City home. He only lasted one term, which is two years.

When he got back to his city, Tweed's social club made him the boss in name and nickname. Social clubs used to be where rich men spent their time relaxing in private rooms, swilling expensive drinks and eating the best food. Eventually, lots of these social clubs became political.

Boss Tweed's social club, the Tammany Society, was no exception. Better known as Tammany Hall, the members fixed elections, put their own men in important jobs around the city, helped Irish immigrants become citizens, and always took a cut of the profits. Most importantly, Tammany was a welfare system before there was one. In a time when immigrants were looked down on, Tammany offered them a way to get involved and move up in life.

Tammany Society:

Tammany was named for a Delaware Native American chief, Tamanend. Legend says he created the Niagara Falls during a battle with evil.

A scared, unsure Irish immigrant could always find a friend in Tammany. And jobs, turkeys at Thanksgiving, **coal at Christmas**, rent money, and even bail money. All the brand-new American citizen had to do was vote exactly as Tammany told him to. Multiple times.

coal at Christmas:

All the good kids wanted coal. They burned it to keep them toasty as marshmallows.

Technically, one person gets one vote. At least, that's the law. But Tammany Hall, and Tweed especially, were very good at breaking the law. During the election of 1868, counters estimated that fifty thousand votes were cast by fake people. How did they know? Because that was way more votes than the number of eligible voters who lived in New York. The Boss couldn't have stolen a city's worth of money without Tammany.

Gaming the System

Money flew to the Boss like he was magnetized. He snapped up real estate, bought printing companies, invested in the stock market (using illegal insider-trading tips, of course), and still found time for his day job—state senator. His most infamous source of money, however, came from graft.

Graft, simply, is political corruption. Tweed abused his political power to make money. In order to get coveted city business contracts (which paid really well), carpenters, plumbers, candlestick makers—anyone who wanted to work on a city project—had to charge the city more money than was strictly necessary on their bills. But the contractor never saw any of that extra money—Tweed did. The extra 15-or-so percent the contractor charged on his bill went straight to Tweed and his Tammany friends.

Tweed and his Tammany cronies with city jobs would only give a contract to a candlestick maker who overcharged the city; later, they'd be the ones to approve the bill and pocket the extra money. It was thievery on a citywide scale. The construction of the **New York County Courthouse** showcased his perfect system.

New York County Courthouse:

Today, it's known as the Tweed Courthouse and currently houses the Department of Education. It's the second-oldest city-government building in Manhattan and is on the National Register of Historic Places.

What was originally a $250,000 budget turned into an $8 million budget, although some say it was closer to $14 million. (That's around $280 million today.) Instead of raising taxes to pay for this suddenly extravagant courthouse and risking angering his people, Tweed's machine just borrowed money from outside of the city and kept it all hush-hush. The city's debt rose from $36 million to $73 million in two years.

Tweed used his ill-gotten gains to play. He bought two steam-powered yachts, his own private entrance to his own private railcar at train stations (to avoid the morning riffraff), luxury houses, a hotel, a railroad, and whatever else his greedy heart fancied. A friend gave him a ten-karat diamond the size of a grape to wear on his suit. He kept all his residences stocked with expensive goody bags to give out magnanimously to friends and enemies alike. Tweed was the real-life winner of the board game Monopoly and he was buying up all those expensive blue squares.

Actually, I run this town.

Boss Tweed wasn't all selfish. Just mostly. He knew that in order to keep himself in charge, he had to keep his people happy. He hosted charity feasts for poor kids and got the ball rolling on special projects for the city—projects like the Metropolitan Museum of Art, the New York Stock Exchange, the Brooklyn Bridge, and the construction of more hospitals and orphanages. He opened up new streets, paved them, put in sewers, and widened Broadway Boulevard. Tweed brought New York's streets out of chaos and into the nineteenth century—streets had fancy lampposts now!

For a guy like Tweed, it was nothing to pay out $100,000 to get his way. In today's money, that's around $2 million. For this amount of cash, the Boss wanted something bigger than sewers. He wanted "Home Rule" of his city.

All the power in the state came from the capital, which wasn't New York City, but Albany, New York. Imagine the popular jock in school being ordered around by his nerdy little brother. That's how New York City felt about Albany controlling everything from their police force to their money. The local New York City government rarely got approval for city improvements, and it infuriated them. Boss Tweed promised to bring the power to New York City. If he could do that, he'd be a hero.

With bags full of cold hard cash, the Boss sat down with fellow Albany politicians. He convinced them to hand over control of New York City to a four-man committee who actually lived in the city. This committee had complete control over the budget, and no one could fire them. It took Tweed about two seconds to make sure the men were Tammany men. He got a cushy new job, too, as one of the four—director of the Public Works Department. Now, he controlled hundreds of jobs and contracts.

Everything was coming up Tweed. He was so popular that when someone tried to joke about erecting a statue of the Boss in a plaza already named after him, people thought that was a great idea and raised ten thousand bucks to do it. The Boss hastily declined. Only the dead should be memorialized with statues. When his enemies in Tammany tried to take him down, Tweed laughed and let them try. By greasing hands and lining pockets with stolen money, anything and everything was going his way.

The Boss looked like Superman—invincible. But every Superman has his kryptonite.

You're going to need to finish my homework ASAP.

Mr. Nasty Strikes Hard

At the height of his popularity, Tweed could fix an election with a twist of his crooked finger, like the 1869 mayoral election when he had the police department bring the ballots to the polls on voting day. It all sounds very official, except there was only one guy to vote for on the ballot—Tweed's guy.

Whenever accusations of thievery made the newspapers, Tweed swatted them away. If political reformers complained, Tweed allowed a committee to investigate his dealings, such as why the construction of the courthouse was taking so long. It cost almost $8,000 to print the report. Probably because the printing company was Tweed's. Even crazier, nobody found anything wrong. It helped that the committee was made up of Tweed friends who all had spotless reputations.

He thought there was nothing and no one money couldn't buy. Unfortunately for Tweed, he underestimated two guys: the political cartoonist Thomas Nast and George Jones, the owner of *The New York Times*.

Charming

What Boss Tweed couldn't buy, he got through using his charm. During the Civil War (1861–65), riots broke out in New York City over the draft. President Lincoln ordered men to join the Union army, but he allowed any man who didn't want to play with his life to buy his way out—for $300. This was an extremely high sum, and only the richest draft evaders could afford it. This made the poor unhappy, and since the poor made up the base of Tammany's support, Tammany wanted to help. Also, the city was tearing itself apart with fighting.

For four days, mobs attacked anything that moved. They looted weapons and marched through the streets killing and burning at will. By the end of the riots, over a hundred people were dead. Troops that had just fought at Gettysburg in the bloodiest battle of the Civil War rushed to New York to put an end to the killing.

During the riots, Tweed walked up and down the streets, trying to calm down people. He knew he'd need a wild plan to match the wild atmosphere. A replacement would be found for anyone called for the draft, including Tweed himself. The replacement would be paid a generous amount to go fight. Lincoln got his warm bodies, and the poor got equal treatment. All Tweed had to do was convince Lincoln to accept the deal.

Whatever happened in Tweed's secret backroom meetings worked. The rioting stopped, and Tammany sent thousands of recruits to Lincoln's army. It was the future Boss's first taste of winning.

Thanks to tattle-tale Jimmy O'Brien, a former Tammany man who hated Tweed, the newspaper had all the dirt it needed to bring down the Boss. Once the newspaper started printing stories about Tweed's secret dealings, Tweed tried offering bribe money. A lot of it.

Both Nast and Jones turned down the chances to be a multimillionaires. Instead, they got together and kept printing a pretty ugly picture of Tweed and Tammany Hall. For days, Jones's *Times* ran stories about the millions of dollars spent on repairs that never happened and the out-of-control budgets on Tweed projects, while Nast drew his nasty cartoons for *Harper's Weekly*. The magazine's readership tripled in only a few weeks.

Nast put words in Tweed's mouth. What could he do about it?

People were outraged. At a time when workers made $2 a day, stealing millions seemed a bit extravagant. A state judge who also used to be a Tweed man suddenly changed course. By his court order, the city shut down its finances so no more money could go to Tweed & Friends. That shutdown included halting payment to city employees. Now, New Yorkers were upset *and* hungry. Tweed paid his Public Works employees out of his own pocket, but that made people even angrier—where had he gotten the money to pay them?

Afraid of a panic that could cripple their economy, European countries refused to trade with New York's Stock Exchange. Tweed's problem was about to become an international crisis. Tweed's two-faced friends were like everyone at a boring party when the chips and dip run out. Gone. No one wanted to walk down the street with him. Some even blackmailed him in exchange for keeping their mouths shut about his thievery.

Future presidential candidate Samuel Tilden put the final nail in Tweed's coffin. He

Samuel Tilden:

He ran as a reform-minded candidate, and used his Tweed takedown to win the popular vote in the 1876 election, but he still lost the presidency to Rutherford B. Hayes.

figured out how the Boss was secretly pocketing the money. Then he made it public. A day later, Tweed was in jail.

By this time, the *friends* portion of Tweed & Friends was long gone. Some fled the country to avoid arrest while others loosened their lips. Only Tweed felt the heat.

The trial was held at the unfinished Tweed Courthouse. Tweed was sentenced to twelve years in prison and slapped with almost $13,000 in fines ($260,000 today), which was really a drop in the ocean of his wealth. The ex-Boss had nicer quarters and better food than the average prisoner, but it was nothing compared to his former Monopoly lifestyle. He had to get out.

Tweed used his favorite party trick—bribery—to make a break for freedom. He ran, sailed, and stayed hidden for ten months, even making it all the way to Spain, but somehow, Nast still thwarted him. Spanish authorities recognized Tweed from Nast's cartoons and turned him back over to American authorities. Tweed tried to cut a deal with the judge by confessing everything, but after he spilled the beans, the judge refused to let him walk. Tweed died in prison, abandoned by everyone but one daughter.

When a big shot goes down, however, there are big ripples. Thanks to Jones and his *Times* articles, papers now exposed corruption instead of endorsing it. Political reformers took over the city, adding checks and balances to those in power. The people that replaced Tweed's cronies in office made huge reforms. People like Andrew Green.

How to kick a guy when he's down.

Green, known for achievements including supporting the creation of the Museum of Natural History, the Bronx Zoo, New York Public Library, Central Park, and incorporating Brooklyn, Queens, and Staten Island into New York City, was also a reformer who cleaned up city jobs. He demanded that employees actually work at work instead of socializing all day, and he banned accepting bribes from candlestick makers. That's just basic practice today, but it was a big reform after Tweed. Green also steadied the city's finances after the free-for-all Tweed had created.

Tammany also changed its spots. In order to avoid the same fate as Tweed, Tammany elected "Honest John" Kelly to clean up their image. He began by enforcing the rules within Tammany ranks, and kept control of New York politics for almost another hundred years.

Boss Tweed stole for himself and because of that, he became the face of corruption, even if his corruption helped the poor in the process. Thanks to him, voters no longer trusted their elected officials to do the right thing with the people's money. They wanted accountability.

To Tweed, he was only doing what so many others in power were doing. Corruption was the name of the game in late-nineteenth-century American politics. Unfortunately for the Boss, he got caught, which meant all the good he did for the city he loved was quickly forgotten, just like the Boss himself. Maybe he should have said yes to that statue after all.

Lived: 1847–1931, America
Occupation: Inventor

Thomas Edison

Not a Hollywood Star

The Wizard

When it comes to Thomas Edison, you might think you've heard it all. He was called the **Wizard of Menlo Park** and performed magical acts, like inventing the light bulb, the phonograph, and the movie camera. Maybe you knew that he had 1,093 **patents** and was a workaholic who rarely clocked out. (When Edison did go home, he'd call reporters to tell the world he worked twice as hard as everyone else.)

But with all that hard work came a bunch of underhanded work, too. Edison was not above using questionable practices we'd frown upon today. That's right. Edison stole. A lot. And it transformed the movie industry.

Lights, camera, action!

> **Wizard of Menlo Park:**
> Edison worked his magic in his laboratory located in Menlo Park, New Jersey.

> **patents:**
> a legal way to protect an invention from anyone trying to copy it.

Name Game

Edison's greatest invention might have been his name. It (and he) were world famous. His inventing laboratories were filled with smart, hardworking underlings who reported directly to Edison, and any of the inventions they created were patented under Edison's name.

One underling, William K. L. Dickson, was a really smart guy. Edison wanted to string together pictures in constant motion and mix in some sound—today, we'd call it a movie. Edison hadn't the foggiest idea how to create this marvel, but it sounded cool. He told Dickson to get to work.

Just peep to see pictures!

Even though he was stressed to the point of collapsing, Dickson got the job done. His kinetograph recorded images on photographic paper, which was then attached to a cylinder. In order to watch the pictures move, a viewer looked through the peephole of the kinetoscope as the images spun around the cylinder. It was a rough, working model, but Edison didn't wait around for perfection. He ran right to the U.S. Patent Office to protect rights to the invention and claimed to the press they'd be watching color television in no time, thanks to him.

Next, Dickson built the first-ever film studio and dubbed it the "Black Maria." The black walls kept all the focus on the actors, and the building revolved to follow the sun, capturing perfect light for recording films.

films:

Edison's guys mostly recorded boxing matches, magic shows, dancers, bodybuilders, acrobats, trained bears, and bits with Buffalo Bill's Wild West show.

Shadow Boxing

When boxers came to the studio, Edison feinted along with them, pretending to throw punches. At the time, however, boxing was technically illegal. When a local judge found out about the matches, Edison was conveniently out of town, and no charges were pressed. Only Edison could get away with such a move!

After a few years of making movies and improvements without any of the credit, Dickson left to form Biograph, his own, rival film company, in 1895. Edison had lost his number-one thinker, and he was pretty bitter about it. Plus, now he had competition.

Pirates on the Video Waves

Today, it's illegal to download movies and music without paying. It's called piracy, and it's stealing. But that's exactly what Edison did. He had to get ahead, because the bottom line (aka, money) was the most important thing to him. Edison was convinced films were just a passing fad, but he wanted to make a bundle while they were still in style.

Edison seated with his underlings. Dickson stands on the left.

The Wizard's first trick: convince competitors they couldn't make a cent and snap up their technology for himself. This only worked a few times, but it's how Edison got his projector screen. Trick two: patent everything he could see, even if he didn't invent it, then sue the pants off anybody who **infringed** on his patents.

infringed: tried to steal something that was patented or under copyright.

This led to a lot of court cases. In fact, Edison was in and out of courts, both suing and being sued, for over twenty years—and that's just for his film patents!

Besides Dickson's Biograph, there were other filmmakers who had the nerve to want to make movies, too. These upstarts had better technology, including better cameras, and they introduced projectors so more people could watch at the same time. Edison sued them for using "his" technology. And being rich and famous gave Edison a competitive edge in court. Sometimes he lost, sometimes he won, but his suing stamina made most film companies fold—except Dickson's.

With so much legal uncertainty, no one want to invest in the film indus-try, including Edison himself. It's not surprising that, instead of spending time, money, and his thinking juices in the uncertain industry *he* created, Edison preferred to steal his movie ideas.

Dupes

Duping is selling an exact copy of a film as your own, and Edison was really good at it. The trick was to be quick, because once a movie was seen, viewers wanted a new one.

In this lawless frontier, Edison was the quickest on the draw. He'd send spies and agents to Europe looking for new films, copy the negatives, then print a bunch more copies to sell as his own films in America.

Méliès's most famous movie, A Trip to the Moon, was duped and remade over and over—even the original negatives were stolen by masked men.

It wasn't just Edison—everyone was doing it. The entire film industry was built on copycatting. European producers were not happy. Especially Georges Méliès. He wrote, directed, and starred in over five hundred films, but he wasn't seeing one franc.

Finally, Méliès sent his brother Gaston to stop all the duping. In 1902, Gaston opened an office in New York and started copyrighting all their work in the U.S.

How was Edison supposed to make money now?

Instead of going straight, Edison went even more crooked. He used secret agents and multiple middlemen to acquire Méliès's prints, and then kept duping and selling them as his own work. Even though Edison was in the middle of suing everybody for duping his material, he kept duping off of them. He wasn't one to not make money!

After years of legal tug-of-war to decide whether duping was fair game or not, the courts finally decided it was illegal. Edison needed to find new **loopholes** for his thievery.

loopholes:

Some loopholes included duping European originals that hadn't been copyrighted in America. Edison had a guy stationed in Europe for just that purpose. In 1904 alone, fifty-five of Edison's eighty-six films were dupes.

Remaking Thievery

Now, Edison's underlings were forced to come up with their own ideas. This led to an array of new narrative techniques, set designs, and acting styles in films, including Edison's most famous film, *The Great Train Robbery*. The first "important" Western was written, directed, and produced by underling Edwin S. Porter in 1903, and it was also the first blockbuster.

American audiences loved American themes. The demand was way greater than the supply. So, Edison found a new way to steal.

Edison's outlaw shoots first, asks questions later. Just like him.

If another company had a successful film, Edison remade it using the same plot, scenes, locations, and dialogue. Then he gave it a new title.

Even though Dickson left Biograph around 1903, the company was still Edison's biggest rival. They'd recently filmed a movie named *Personal*, about a Frenchman looking for a rich American wife. Before Biograph was able to release it, Edison's team quickly remade it. The only major thing they changed was the title: *How a French Nobleman Got a Wife Through the New York Herald Personal Columns*. Catchy, right? Audiences thought so. They preferred Edison's version over Biograph's, even though it was the same movie in all but name.

This, of course, led to more court cases and more years of litigation, but Edison won again. Finally, all the other filmmakers couldn't take it anymore.

Fast and Furious

When Edison couldn't get his greedy hands on a copy of Biograph's *Personal*, he stole their employees, instead, putting them to work remaking it, even though the original wasn't even out yet! Sadly for Biograph, audiences preferred Edison's techniques, and *Personal* was a flop. So Biograph sued.

Edison's defense: we may have used the same scenes, plots, characters, and locations, but the camera angles were different. And the lighting. And the title.

This seems like silly stuff and would definitely count as piracy today, but it led to serious questions. Could a film producer "own" a genre? In *Personal*, there were funny moments and a chase scene. Could only Biograph have the right to write about chases or use certain jokes? Where would Hollywood be without comedies or the *Fast and Furious* franchise?

The judge reviewing the *Biograph v. Edison* case decided there were enough things different that it wasn't a straight imitation, even though it would be by today's standards. Remakes became a way to get creative—even though everything else was the same, other aspects did have to change (like camera techniques). Moviemakers were forced to think outside the box, which propelled the industry forward even faster. Today, you have to check the copyright notice and get the rights to remake any film you love, but remakes are still very popular in Hollywood.

Mission to Monopolize

The filmmakers who were still around—including Méliès—were tired of being dragged to court by Edison. They got together and decided that if they couldn't beat him, they'd join him.

Edison loved control, so this was perfect. His company was now in charge of all the other film companies, which is called a monopoly. Edison's umbrella corporation was called the Motion Picture Patents Company (MPPC). At first, Biograph had refused to join, so Edison sued again. And again. And again. Each time, Edison changed the wording just a little in his lawsuit. Finally, Biograph was too tired to fight and was sick of wasting time and money in court. They decided to negotiate.

By this time, movies were becoming a wildly popular form of entertainment. They were magic, and the Wizard was delivering new films every day of the week. (Except Sundays.) Some filmmakers were producing up to five films a week for the MPPC!

time:
Practically every street corner shop housed a backroom movie theater when Edison's monopoly formalized in December 1908.

Like a protective guard dog, Edison didn't like anyone new moving in on his territory. The MPPC hired thugs to sniff out independent filmmakers' studios and smash their cameras and projectors. They beat up other filmmakers and set fire to theaters. No one operated without getting Edison's approval and writing a big, fat check to the Wizard. He was making over a million dollars a year from MPPC profits!

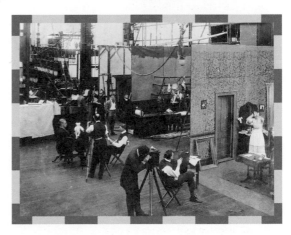

Several Films in Production (1907)

Condensed CliffsNotes®

After Edison cornered the market, he had to think up new ways to steal. His filmmakers began a new form of thievery: adaptions.

Today, we love watching our favorite books become movies. So did people a hundred years ago. Filmmakers took five-hundred-page books and cut them down to highlights reels. Audiences everywhere were thrilled. Book publishers were not.

In 1911, a huge case finally went to the Supreme Court—the highest law in the land. One of the smaller companies in Edison's monopoly, Kalem, had turned the huge novel *Ben-Hur* into a fifteen-minute film. They weren't trying to fool anybody into thinking it was their original idea—to even understand what was going on, audiences had to already know the story. But the book publisher was not happy. They weren't getting a cut!

spectacle:
something that attracts attention because it's weird or shocking.

Edison coughed up money to pay Kalem's legal defenses. In the long run, doing so would be a lot cheaper than paying publishers for the copyrights of all the plays and books he wanted to adapt. Kalem argued that the film was just **spectacle** and not worthy of being copyrighted. And anyway, they were practically giving away free advertisement for the book. After seeing Kalem's adaption, viewers would race to buy the book from stores!

The court didn't agree. They ruled that filmmakers had to pay for the right to remake a book. Thanks to a stolen movie idea, the film industry (and publishing industry!) was changed all over again.

Spectacular!

Wondering why it took the courts so long to outlaw unauthorized adaptions? Mostly because adaptations were considered "spectacle." To these judges, making a show of showing off was not enough to be worthy of a copyright. Dancing girls, strongmen, and other circus-type acts all fell under the umbrella of spectacle.

Two Thieves in a Pod

The *Ben-Hur* decision changed the copyright game and forced filmmakers to start thinking up completely new stories. That was more energy than Edison was willing to use, but **independent filmmakers** loved it!

independent filmmakers: *anybody not signed on to Edison's monopoly.*

Using Edison cameras without permission and black-market film paper to make their own films, the independents created longer movies that featured big star power. Edison didn't want to change with the times. He preferred stock characters and stories, because that was quicker and easier. His company couldn't keep up with demand either. That didn't mean he was going to let these upstarts steal from him!

The Wizard pulled out his favorite trick from his magic hat: lengthy lawsuits. Edison went back to suing everyone in the film business for using "his" technology without paying him what he wanted.

The independents didn't hang around. California was calling with its year-round sunshine, cheap land, labor, and lack of Edison. They fled west where it was as lawless as they were. If Edison's thugs came looking for their paychecks now, filmmakers could hop across the Mexican border for a quick tropical getaway.

As a result, a little thing called Hollywood was born.

The End

Edison had had enough of the movies. Sure, they'd blown up bigger than he ever dreamed possible, but he was out. They were too low-brow for him, anyway with all their shoot-em-up scenes and low-speed car chases.

The courts were starting to crack down on him, and the independents had changed the game with all their original ideas in sunny locales. Edison was interested in other things and always bouncing to the next big idea. Like a phone that could chat with ghosts!

Even worse for the media mogul, as part of a crusade to help the common man, President Theodore Roosevelt had started busting up monopolies to give smaller businesses a chance. By 1915, the courts had tied Edison's MPPC to a railroad track and crushed it, just like in the movies. They declared it an illegal trade "conspiracy." The Wizard said goodbye and good riddance.

Edison's damsel is distressed.

Edison didn't care about making movie magic or entertaining the masses, as much as he was fascinated by the science behind making pictures move, and *super* fascinated by the money it made. But really, it was his thievery that helped create a new form of mass entertainment—going to the movies. By his death in 1931, the movies were an industry in their own right.

Studios like Universal, MGM, and Paramount were already raking in millions from blockbusters like *Frankenstein* and *Mata Hari*, starring A-list celebs including Charlie Chaplin and Greta Garbo, and the Academy Awards (Oscars) were already giving out shiny bald men. The movies that Edison helped steal into existence were now in the hands of the people.

The end.

Copyright or Wrong?

Today, new technology keeps advancing at the speed of a projector light, and the courts have trouble keeping up with all the inventions.

To combat lawlessness, copyright laws keep being updated, and as one film historian says, "piracy is often just a name for media practices we have yet to figure out how to regulate." We're not talking about recording a movie on your cellphone in a theater and then trying to sell admission to your recording—everyone agrees that's illegal. But what about all the other gray areas, like putting words across well-known photographs to create funny memes? Those aren't your photos! Or dubbing over scenes in films with your own dialogue? Hilarious! And illegal. But, just like Edison, people have always found that loopholes and copyright laws are purposefully written with vague words to allow wiggle room.

So, where should artistic freedom end and the law begin?

Lived: 1881–1925, Italy and France
Occupation: Handyman

Vincenzo Peruggia

Details, Details, Details

V for Vincenzo. And Vendetta.

Vincenzo Peruggia was not a criminal mastermind. He didn't want to be eternally famous or take over the world. More importantly, he didn't have the talent necessary for a life of crime. He'd inhaled one too many paint fumes for that.

Vincenzo, an Italian immigrant, had been living in Paris for over two years doing odd jobs. One day it would be house painting; the next, carpentry. He was a bit of a Renaissance man, just like his Italian homeboy, Leonardo da Vinci. Unlike Leonardo, however, Vincenzo's talents weren't making him famous, just a little bit **crazy**.

Life in France for Vincenzo stunk. The Eiffel Tower wasn't romantic when he visited it by himself, and he missed his mom's cooking. The French weren't warm and welcoming, either.

crazy:

Paint before 1978 contained lead, a highly toxic chemical that can affect the brain.

They called him "**macaroni**" and didn't invite him to their bistros for wine and cheese parties.

Vincenzo tried to ignore it all and keep working. For eight months, the Louvre Museum in Paris employed Vincenzo as a *glazier*. That gave him plenty of time to glare at all the Italian art locked behind French doors.

The imprisoned Italian art was all thanks to that grouse Napoleon (see chapter 5), who had looted Italy over a hundred years before. It made Vincenzo's insides burn just thinking about it—even more than getting called a common pasta shape.

> **macaroni:**
> This wasn't a nice thing to call someone from Italy.

> **glazier:**
> A person who works with glass, including cutting it and placing it in frames.

Vincenzo figured Leonardo da Vinci's beautiful *Mona Lisa* was part of Napoleon's plunder. That made Vincenzo really angry, and he decided to do something about it. Forget about the fact that the *Mona Lisa* had been completed in France and Leonardo's heir sold it to the French king, François I, long before Napoleon raided Italy. Vincenzo believed the painting belonged in Italy.

Although Peruggia wasn't working for the Louvre anymore, the handyman had everything he needed to execute his plan: a white worker's smock to blend in, knowledge of the museum's layout, and a good ole fashioned vendetta to fuel his anger. The *Mona Lisa* would see Italian soil again!

A Painting and a Glazier Walk into a Stairwell . . .

The Louvre made Vincenzo's art heist easier than taking candy from a baby. Everything was low-tech at the Louvre in 1911. All the great works of art hung from hooks on the wall. That way, if there was a fire, workers could run through the halls and grab the frames while sprinting to safety.

The museum also had no alarms or surveillance systems. When a worker wanted to remove a painting for cleaning, they didn't have to sign it out. If there was a big gap where a painting usually hung, most workers assumed it was getting photographed for publicity or having a spa day for routine maintenance.

Heartbreaker

The number of guards, too, was on the low side. During regular museum hours, the Salon Carré, the room where the *Mona Lisa* lived, had only one guard, who was also in charge of two other rooms. On Mondays when the museum was closed, there were only twelve guards to patrol over four hundred rooms.

So that's how Vincenzo found himself staring at the painting on a Monday morning in August 1911. With no one around, he plucked the framed painting off the hooks and hightailed it out of the gallery.

Renaissance paintings weren't done on canvases. They were painted on wooden boards, so Vincenzo couldn't roll up the *Mona Lisa* and walk out cool as a cannoli. He had to take the board, wrap his smock around it, and hope no one noticed the *Mona Lisa*–shaped package under his arm. Luckily for him, he ran into no one as he made his escape.

He lugged his lady to a service stairwell and tried the door, which was locked. What was a criminal mastermind wannabe **to do**?

While perhaps not as exciting as rappelling out a window or BASE jumping to freedom, Vincenzo decided on the easiest path. He came out exactly the way he went in—the front door.

Spoofing with Sfumato

Leonardo da Vinci is literally the definition of a Renaissance man. If Leonardo didn't know it, he learned it—from flying contraptions, to human anatomy, to art. While designing diving suits and armored cars is a pretty cool legacy, it's Leonardo's mastery of painting techniques that transformed the world.

Sfumato means "to vanish into smoke" (*fuma*), and Leonardo perfected it with his smoky backgrounds. His next technique, *chiaroscuro*, amped up the drama. Picture a spotlight on a lone actor standing on a black stage. Leonardo did this with paint for his subjects, and it was pretty innovative for a time when most portraits looked more like Sunday morning cartoons than real people.

Louvre curator Jean-Pierre Cuzin says Leonardo's sense of style influenced every single portrait after the *Mona Lisa*. From Dutch masters to Picasso, they all owe a little something to the mysterious Lady and her creator.

---

to do:

He tried removing the doorknob, but the lock was on the actual door. Taking off the knob just left him staring into a tiny hole of freedom. He later tossed the knob outside the Louvre.

He freed his lady from behind her glass cage (which he knew exactly how to do, being a glazier), left the frame behind, and walked into the morning sunshine with the small, wooden picture wrapped in a white smock tucked under his arm.

It was a perfect crime. Fantasies of fame, fortune, and maybe even a National Vincenzo Day followed Peruggia back to his apartment. The world—well, Italy—would love him for saving the *Mona Lisa*. He'd be a hero. He just had to bide his time and wait for everything to cool down in Paris before sneaking her out of the country, because he was pretty sure France wouldn't be happy with him.

He was right. He just didn't know how right.

How to Get Famous

On Tuesday, the museum thought someone was playing a not-so-funny prank on them. The director was on holiday, so the back-up guy decided to close the museum due to a "broken water pipe." When the *Mona Lisa* didn't walk herself back in all day, the back-up director decided the police should be notified. Later that night, the Louvre finally broke the news. It wasn't until Wednesday that anyone took it seriously.

People in Paris were dismayed. Newsboys screamed, *"C'est partie!"* which means, "She has left!" Even though the Louvre was closed for the next week, thousands came to lay flowers at the gates and wrote obituaries for the painting as if its subject had died. Newspapers made her absence their front-page story. The entire world mourned for their missing Mona Lisa.

Everyone wanted to help find her, probably because of the impressive reward being offered by the newspaper, *Paris-Journal*. Tips flooded in. It seemed everyone and their uncle had seen the *Mona Lisa* at some point in a dream, on a boat, riding a train, or walking down the street. Fortune tellers offered their services, although one insisted the painting had been destroyed.

The Louvre refused to give up hope. They ran an experiment. First, they asked a policeman to remove a replica *Mona Lisa* from its frame. It took him more than five minutes of awkward wiggling. When they asked a worker, it took six seconds—and that included leaving the room with the painting in hand. They concluded it had to be an inside job. So far, so good.

Next, they called in Alphonse Bertillon, the French Sherlock Holmes, to help investigate. He was famous in a CSI way. Bertillon is credited with taking the first mugshots and creating a whole system of identifying repeat criminals based on their physical appearance. In fact, he was the first detective in Europe to catch a murderer based on fingerprints alone.

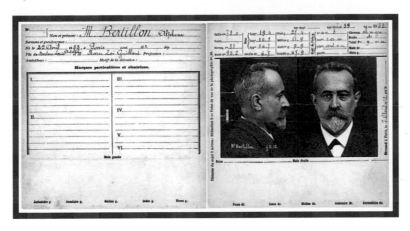

Bertillon himself, posing for his mugshot.

Bertillon carefully lifted one intact fingerprint from the frame. *Bingo!* He sifted through hundreds of prints taken from current and former Louvre employees, but he wasn't able to identify the print on the frame as Vincenzo's. Vincenzo even had a print on file at the police station from a previous arrest, but Bertillon never matched it. That was bad luck, but police still visited all former employees for a quick interrogation—really quick.

Before the police came calling, Vincenzo had hidden his lady in a suitcase with a trapdoor bottom. Nothing fancy, just his underwear to keep the *Mona Lisa* company. The *Mona Lisa* had hung out in King Francis I's bathroom for a while, too. She was used to underwear. (And Napoleon's bedroom! See chapter 5.)

Despite sitting a few feet away from the missing painting, investigators still couldn't close the case. They didn't thoroughly search the apartment, however, because some scholars think the investigators didn't believe a working-class foreigner could have masterminded the disappearing act.

The investigation was back to square one.

The Louvre fired directors, their head of security, and a few guards, but it didn't bring the *Mona Lisa* back. Police detained anybody who looked

Pablo Picasso:

He didn't dirty his own hands in the theft, but hired Géry Pieret to snatch the statues. Picasso used them as a model for the painting that was his first foray into Cubism: Les Demoiselles d'Avignon. When he wasn't keeping them in his sock drawer.

suspicious, including famous artist **Pablo Picasso**. It turned out that Picasso did steal a few statues from the Louvre for inspiration, but not the *Mona Lisa*. Eventually, the Louvre had no choice but to admit defeat. The museum reopened with a large blank spot where the *Mona Lisa* had once hung. Thousands of people flocked to stare at an empty space on the wall.

Before Vincenzo stole her, the *Mona Lisa* was sort of famous in the same way a B-list celebrity is famous. People knew of her, but she wasn't even the most valuable painting in the Louvre, let alone the world. She'd even been criticized for having "hands more alive than (her) head!"

corsets:

Stiff garments worn around the torso to torture wearers into better posture and skinnier waistlines.

Now, all levels of society knew about her. From dictators to taxi drivers, no one could resist talking about Mona Lisa. People created postcards of her travels, told love stories about her and her captor, and used her face to sell everything from cigarettes to **corsets**.

But as the months dragged by, other news stories started to replace her highness, like the sinking of the Titanic eight months later. People got bored of all the false sightings of the painting and slowly, the world gave up hope of finding her.

Vincenzo couldn't have been happier.

There's a Raphael around the corner. . . .

She's Ready for Her Close-up

For over two years, Peruggia waited for people to forget about the *Mona Lisa* theft, and, eventually, they did. Now it was time for his grand reveal.

Most important for the reveal was the location: Mona Lisa's close-up needed to happen on Italian soil where she belonged (or so Vincenzo thought).

Two years is a lot of time to gain perspective. When Vincenzo wrote to art dealer Alfredo Geri that he had the *Mona Lisa* and wanted to debut her in her home country, he also mentioned that he didn't really want any money, but baguettes didn't grow on trees. Some lire would help. Not one for subtlety, Vincenzo signed the letter "Leonardo" and waited for a response.

lire:
Italian money

Geri thought the letter had about as much credibility as a grainy picture of Bigfoot. He made fun of it before almost throwing it away. *Almost.* After a little more thought, Geri decided it might be the real deal. Who was still pretending they had the *Mona Lisa* after all this time?

Geri wrote back telling the thief not to worry about the money and that his friend, Director Poggi of the Uffizi Gallery, wanted to tag along. Director Poggi kept a Leonardo in his museum and would help authenticate her.

It was *au revoir*, Paris. Vincenzo packed his underwear in the false-bottomed suitcase and made a beeline for Florence. "Leonardo" met the experts at his hotel room, where he dumped out broken shoes, a hat that had been sat upon, tools, and a violin to expose the suitcase's false bottom. Then, as the two experts held their breath, Vincenzo revealed the lady. Considering she'd been on the run for two years, it was really lucky that the *Mona Lisa* only had two little scratches.

Director Poggi knew the real thing when he saw it, but he didn't tell that to Vincenzo. Instead, he asked to take the painting to his gallery so that he might compare it to other works by Leonardo. Once there, Poggi promptly locked his door and called the police.

Director Poggi (on right) eyeballing the elusive smile on the elusive lady.

Vincenzo stayed in his hotel room and waited for his reward money. He got handcuffs instead.

Vincenzo was a bit surprised at the rough treatment he received, but figured it was just a formality. Once the people of Italy heard his story, they would hail him as a hero. After all, he wasn't a thief; he was a patriot who had abducted the *Mona Lisa* in order to make up for the plunder-fest Napoleon had carried out a century before! Who would dare call that criminal?

His fan club didn't. Vincenzo was right about one thing—Italy loved him. People sent money, cigarettes, and food to his prison cell while he waited patiently to be vindicated. And then he waited . . . and waited . . . and waited.

Six months and one **psychiatrist** later, Vincenzo finally got his day in court. Everyone knew he'd stolen the *Mona Lisa*; that wasn't the question. The Italian court only wanted to determine if he'd done it for Italy, as he'd claimed, or for the lire he was sure he'd receive.

Vincenzo's defense insisted no harm had been done. If anything, Vincenzo had helped the world. France saw how weak their security was, and Italy got to see the beautiful lady. Still, the judge had to do something, so he sentenced Vincenzo to one year and fifteen days in jail. The sentence was later reduced to seven months, all of which the thief had already served.

Vincenzo walked onto the Italian soil a free man seven months and nine days after his arrest, unlike the *Mona Lisa*, which had long been returned to her gilded cage in France.

psychiatrist:

When an expert was sent in to verify Peruggia's mental health, Vincenzo didn't pass the sanity test. The expert decided that the house painter was "intellectually deficient."

Not a Fan of the Renaissance?

Since her 1911 theft, the *Mona Lisa* has been vandalized multiple times. As a result, she is encased in bulletproof glass in a virtual bunker. So don't even *think* about it. There are better ways to get a day named after you.

Here's a list of the attacks:

- 1956: Acid damaged the lower left half of the canvas.
- 1956: A thrown rock chipped the paint on her elbow.
- 1974: Red spray paint vandalized the protective glass.
- 2009: A thrown terracotta mug from the museum gift shop shattered against the glass.

An Untouchable Icon

Mona Lisa may have left the Louvre on the B-list, but when she came back, there wasn't a list that could hold her. Starting with a triumphant tour of Italy, *Mona Lisa* recaptured the hearts of millions. Wherever she went, stampedes broke out and riot police had to be called. The world had caught *Mona Lisa* madness. Suddenly, she was the most famous work of art in the world, and now she belonged to the world. At least, her image did. Her face changed the world of mass art even though her actual face was stuck in France.

People put her now-iconic smile on everything, making her the first mass-produced image on a global scale. Suddenly, she was everywhere, and as a result, people loved her. Women dusted themselves with yellow makeup powder to achieve her golden glow. Excited viewers lined up around the city to see her home. She returned to the Louvre in a custom-padded box—underwear not included—with an honor guard twenty policemen deep.

Art for the masses—that's you!

The Louvre also got an upgrade. Paintings had to be signed out before being taken for restoration. More guards were posted in the galleries, and contractors like Peruggia were photographed for the museum security's files.

Selfie!

The *Mona Lisa* has come a long way from Vincenzo's suitcase. Today, the *Mona Lisa* madness continues with her face parading across billboards, coffee mugs, umbrellas, and even toilet paper. If you can think it, the *Mona Lisa* can adorn it.

As for the lady herself, she lives in a bulletproof case, has her own bodyguards, and a **Do-Not-Remove** policy. She's French forever. Vincenzo, on the other hand, didn't get the reward money, but he did get plenty of love from his fellow Italians.

Maybe he was a criminal mastermind after all.

Do-Not-Remove:

Except for that time when First Lady Jackie Kennedy got her on U.S. soil in 1963 to show to the American people, and a quick world tour in 1974 where excited viewers were given ten seconds to ogle her before being shuffled along.

Lived: 1911–1988, Europe, America
Occupation: Physicist, Spy

Klaus Fuchs

An Explosive Thinker

The Real Deal

On August 29, 1949, the Soviet Union scared the protons out of the world when they tested an atomic bomb. It'd been four years since America had detonated their own atomic bomb during World War II, but everyone was still shocked. How in science's sake had the Russians figured it out so quickly?

This is it: the spy story you've been waiting for. It has code names, explosions, stolen information, late night meet-ups, and a world at risk. (Although, just so you know, there are a lot fewer fancy tuxedos and fast cars in the real spy world. Most of spies' work involves standing on street corners, eating from questionable hot-dog stands, and being alone. A lot.)

This is the story of Klaus Fuchs, code name "Charles"—the atomic spy of the century.

Pretty much how you pictured him, right?

It's REALLY Not Rocket Science

Klaus Fuchs was a nerd. Nobody would deny that. In fact, everyone who met him called him an "intellectual" type, which is code for nerd. You don't even have to be a spy to figure that one out.

Fuchs joined a gang of boys as a teenager while growing up in Germany in the 1920s. At that time, the Nazis were just starting their reign of terror against anyone they didn't like. That included the Fuchs family. They weren't Jewish, but they were still on the Nazi radar for being communists.

Fuchs's new friends hated the Nazis as much as he did. They threw sticks and stones at them in street fights. But in 1933, Fuchs had to flee. Hitler had taken power and started a campaign to get rid of everyone who didn't fit his definition of a perfect human being; that included Jews, communists, disabled people, and a whole lot of others. His father, brother, and one of his sisters weren't as lucky, and they either committed suicide or were thrown in concentration camps by the Nazis. Eventually, Fuchs found himself in England, studying and writing impressive-sounding papers on subjects like nuclear theory.

It seemed like a perfect fit—after all, the English government hated the Nazis taking over Germany, too. Fuchs was so happy to be there, he wanted to become a British citizen! Until Britain threw him into an internment camp. Once World War II started, they weren't sure how to tell who was a Nazi sympathizer and who was just German. They decided to be scared of *all* Germans.

Fuchs found himself in the prison-like camp, writing his impressive papers with thousands of other Germans. They slept in sheds and did their business in six bathrooms for every 720 people. It doesn't take a quantum scientist to know why he turned to the Soviet Union (USSR).

When Harry Met Fuchs

A bunch of smart people got together and protested Fuchs being locked up. It worked, and he was released to work on behalf of the war effort. For the next three years, Fuchs researched the British atomic bomb, and the whole time, he told the Soviets **everything he knew**, which wasn't a lot. Figuring out how to split atoms to make them explode was hard work and the British hadn't gotten far. But Fuchs did tell the Soviets enough to make them worried and to start their own research.

everything he knew:

Fuchs and other spies for the Soviet Union believed Britain should have given up the bomb information freely because allies were technically supposed to share. Instead, Britain made Fuchs sign the Official Secrets Act when he started working on the bomb to keep his mouth shut.

When America joined the war, the Brits and Americans decided to work together on the atom bomb. The Soviets were not invited, and they were not happy. Weren't they all allies against the Nazis?

By this time, Fuchs had gotten his British citizenship. The Brits didn't know about his double life; he was too smart to be caught. In fact, Fuchs was so smart, he was part of the British team sent to New York to work with Americans to figure out the atom-bomb secrets. Of course, he told the Soviets all about his new assignment.

In December 1943, he arrived in New York City to join the **Manhattan Project**. By February 1944, he had his first meeting with his American **handler**, Harry Gold.

Manhattan Project:

The Allies' top secret project to create a working atomic bomb.

The first time Harry met Fuchs, it was sort of awkward. Fuchs stood on a street corner in the middle of winter holding a tennis ball and a green book, while Harry carried some extra gloves. Gold approached and asked, "What is the way to Chinatown?" Fuchs was supposed to say, "I think Chinatown closes at five o'clock." That was it. The spies were in contact.

handler:

A person in charge of handling spies active in the field. Harry Gold, an American Jew working for the USSR, handled Fuchs's information and passed it to his Soviet handlers, who passed it back to Joseph Stalin, head of the Soviet Union.

Harry said his name was "Raymond" and treated Fuchs to a nice steak dinner. Fuchs was

This tennis ball isn't obvious at all in the dead of winter. . . .

not impressed. They were spies! They were supposed to be low-key! Harry got the memo: this wasn't Fuchs's first rodeo.

The next time they met, in March, Fuchs brushed past Gold, slipping him a huge packet of information. Gold couldn't resist—he peeked. It was a lot of math. Gold knew he was holding gold. Over the next few months, they met six times. Then suddenly, Fuchs didn't show.

Weapons of Mass Destruction

After some frantic detective work, Fuchs's handlers figured out he had been sent to Los Alamos, New Mexico—the belly of the beast. The Manhattan Project wasn't just theoretical research anymore, and New Mexico was the perfect place to test this new weapon of mass destruction.

Security was tight. There was barbed wire, limited communications, and special passes for any worker wanting to leave the compound. Everything was on a need-to-know basis. Mostly, nobody needed to know what anybody else was working on. Fuchs spent the majority of his time on calculations for how big a boom the bombs would make.

Fuchs wasn't able to get a pass off the premises to see his family until February 1945. His next meeting with Gold was at Fuchs's sole surviving sister's house in Cambridge, Massachusetts. Fuchs gave Gold another packet of information about the bomb design, critical mass, lenses, and other scientific information. They set their next meeting in New Mexico for the summer. Then Gold tried to give Fuchs money. Fuchs turned him down. He was doing this to stop the Nazis. Period.

Oh, That Bomb

Although they were technically allies working together, the United States thought Stalin and his Soviet Union were scary. As the war was coming to a close, the three allies—America, Britain, and the Soviet Union—all met at Potsdam, Germany, to discuss Europe's fate after the war. President Truman let it "slip" to Stalin that the U.S. had successfully tested the world's first atomic weapon. Hint, hint: so play nice around the U.S.

Stalin's (imagined) response: "Oh, a super destructive, game-changing bomb? Great. Sounds wonderful."

Truman seemed a little surprised that Stalin wasn't more surprised. That's because the Soviet leader already knew all about it thanks to his spies like Fuchs.

"Friends" getting together at Potsdam.

Code-named Trinity, the first test of a nuclear weapon.

In June, they met on a bridge over the Santa Fe River in Fuchs's beat-up, blue Buick. He handed over the design of the atomic bomb. For a while, Fuchs thought it would never be finished in time to use in the war. He knew better now.

Two months later, the United States dropped the first nuclear bombs to be deployed during war on the Japanese cities of Hiroshima on August 6th, 1945, and Nagasaki on August 9th, 1945. Life on earth would never be the same.

What's in a Bomb?

Both the A-bomb and the H-bomb are types of nuclear weapons, because they involve nuclear reactions. Here are their differences:

- Atomic bomb: The atomic bomb (A-bomb) is a type of nuclear bomb that uses fission (the splitting apart of an atom) to create huge amounts of energy.
- Thermonuclear bomb: This is the hydrogen bomb (H-bomb), which works by fusion (smashing together parts of atoms). The process of fusion starts with fission, so the H-bomb has an A-bomb at its core. There can be multiple layers of this fission/fusion action, which scientists have compared to a layer cake. Depending on how many layers the bomb contains, it can create energy thousands of times more powerful than an A-bomb. The largest H-bomb ever exploded was by the Soviet Union in 1961, and was thought to have had three layers. This explosion equaled fifty million tons of TNT.

Not So Super

The war was over, but the work wasn't done. Having one type of nuclear weapon wasn't enough; the Americans had been simultaneously working on a second type—a thermonuclear weapon. While the atomic bomb was extremely devastating, killing hundreds of thousands of people and releasing damaging radiation in its wake, the hydrogen bomb, a thermonuclear weapon nicknamed the "Super," had the capacity to be infinitely worse.

Now that America had detonated a nuclear weapon, world peace wasn't magically restored. In fact, many, including Fuchs, thought it was at even greater risk. He believed that no country should have so much power, because it created an imbalance. The only answer to him was to keep giving information to the Soviets in order to keep everyone on even footing.

Luckily for Fuchs, he was in New Mexico where he still had access to information. Unluckily for Fuchs, now that the war was over, the Americans didn't want to share all their secrets with the British. He was asked to research radiation poisoning instead.

Finally, in April 1946, Fuchs was able to attend a conference on the Super. He also accepted a job back in **England**, working on British nuclear weapons. The Brits considered Fuchs so vital, they flew him across the Atlantic on a bomber plane instead of having him take the usual long boat ride.

England:

Fuchs was stationed at a research facility in Harwell, England, in the third-highest position. There was still nuclear research going on at Harwell into the 1990s.

After settling into his new gig, Fuchs did the only thing he thought was right: he contacted the Soviets. This time it wasn't nearly as awkward as his first encounter with Gold had been.

His new handler, Soviet spy Alexander Feklisov, met Fuchs in a pub. He later recalled that Fuchs gave off a nerdy scientist vibe from a mile away. Fuchs sat reading the *Tribune* newspaper, and Feklisov carried a red book. Once they determined no one was tailing them, Feklisov was supposed to say, "The stout is not as it should be. I prefer lager." Fuchs was supposed to reply, "Nothing can compare to Guinness." Success!

From September 1947 to April 1949, the two spies met every three to four months. Feklisov would receive Fuchs's handwritten notes on the British progress, copy it, and ship it to the Soviet Union. Sometimes they met in the pub. Other times they met in dark movie theaters.

America was still confident the Soviets were seven to eight years away from setting off their own nuclear bombs. They didn't know what Fuchs knew: that the Soviets only needed a year or two.

Then, on August 29, 1949, the Soviets tested their first A-bomb, shocking pretty much everyone but themselves. America and Britain were so suspicious, they immediately launched an investigation into the matter. Both decided the Soviets could never have reached the bomb so fast without inside information.

Women breaking Soviet spy codes like glass ceilings.

Codebreakers deciphered Soviet spy messages in a secret program called the Venona Project. Some spy the Soviets called "Charles" seemed responsible.

The hunt was on for the atomic spy in the Manhattan Project.

It's Getting Hot in Here

It took about as long as it takes an atom to split—which isn't very long at all—before the FBI was on to the nerdy British scientist. By September 1949, the FBI had already pinpointed Fuchs and told the Brits. They also got super serious about figuring out the hydrogen bomb's secrets.

thermonuclear party:

The fusion process for the hydrogen bomb begins at fifty million degrees Celsius. In comparison, the center of the sun is a cool fifteen million degrees Celsius.

Nobody wanted to be the last one to the hottest party of the century—the **thermonuclear party**. Because of all the anxiety around suspected spies in general and Fuchs in particular, the Americans were convinced he had given the USSR the secrets to the atomic bomb, the hydrogen bomb, and maybe even the universe. To stay one step ahead, President Truman ordered the hydrogen bomb built on January 31, 1950.

The obvious next move would have been to arrest Fuchs and stop all that secret-sharing. Instead, the Brits kept calm and let him carry on with his work. To keep him from getting suspicious, they gave him a raise and a bigger apartment. Of course, they tapped his phone, followed his movements, and opened his mail, too. It wasn't until December that they brought him in for some friendly questioning—with expert secret-getter William Skardon.

Skardon and Fuchs played cat-and-mouse games with each other over coffee and cigarettes for a month. Fuchs seemed tired of spying and didn't like the direction the Soviet Union was headed. They seemed bent on power, just like America. Fuchs also admitted that he'd gotten used to life in Britain, and it was pretty cushy. As for his handler, Feklisov thought maybe Fuchs considered his job was done once the Soviets caught up and set off their own bomb. He was ready to leave the game.

Whatever the real motivation, Fuchs confessed to espionage in late January 1950. Aside from the arms race his spying had heated up, and the **Red Scare** his arrest had helped start, Fuchs's confession also brought down the two most notorious spies in the atomic business, Julius and Ethel Rosenberg.

> **Red Scare:**
>
> Also known as McCarthyism, the Red Scare was about rooting out all suspected communists in the United States. Senator Joseph McCarthy announced one week after Fuchs's arrest that there were probably over two hundred communists working in America's government, scaring everyone.

Atomic World

People started to worry their next-door neighbors could be Soviet spies, and the hysteria spread. To understand how big the spy ring was, the FBI needed to know who Fuchs had worked with in America, so they went after his handler like a proton chasing an electron. They drew up lists with thousands of names fitting Fuchs's description of his American handler: short, plump, and white. That fit about half the men in America.

After a few rounds of trial and error, they started showing pictures of men to Fuchs. Finally, in May 1950, he positively identified Harry Gold from a video after lying and saying it wasn't him a few times. At the same time in

The doomed Rosenbergs

America, Gold was confessing as well to lessen his "horrible sense of shame." And just like Fuchs, Gold didn't try to escape. He was arrested immediately.

The Soviet Union went into damage control. They tried getting their agents out of Britain and the United States, but it was way too late. Gold was a goldmine, and he was bringing everyone down with him. The FBI admitted he gave them so much information, they couldn't keep up with the workload!

He implicated another contact from New Mexico, David Greenglass, who was so desperate to save his skin and his wife's that he threw out his sister's name, Ethel, and her husband, Julius Rosenberg. In all of the hysteria of communism and the Soviet Union in the 1950s, the Rosenbergs had no chance—the judge blamed them for the Korean War and the death of fifty thousand Americans. Then he sentenced them to death. On June 19, 1953, they were sent to the electric chair. Most historians today believe that Julius was certainly a spy, but that Ethel probably wasn't, and she only knew about his behavior and, at most, approved of it.

As for Fuchs, he was sentenced to fourteen years. He only served nine before he was released early for good behavior, like organizing a school for the other inmates. After he got out, Fuchs went to East Germany to become a professor and died there in 1988.

Despite the FBI's fears, Fuchs didn't have all the answers to all the problems. That's why he continued to research and learn. However, he was the closest of all the researchers to figuring out how to make the hydrogen bomb tick.

Fuchs and another "intellectual type," John Von Neumann, applied for a secret patent on a design to help set off the hydrogen bomb back in 1946. It wasn't used in the final design, but that's because technology hadn't advanced far enough yet to make it happen. Fuchs still passed it on to the Soviets, who couldn't use it either.

John Von Neumann:

Another great scientific mind who fled the Nazis in Europe, because he was Jewish. Not only did Von Neumann help with nuclear weapons research, he also was a key creator of game theory.

It's not certain how many years Fuchs helped take off the Soviet bomb construction. Some scientists believe ten years, while others are more moderate in their estimate at one or two. Either way, his boss in New Mexico, Hans Bethe, called Fuchs "the only physicist I know who truly changed history." And Bethe knew Albert Einstein. That's a pretty impressive name to sit above.

The Soviets also appreciated Fuchs's expertise, but not until they were sure he was dead. They mentioned his name for the first time only months after his funeral. From East Germany, he received the Order of Karl Marx, the highest civilian honor they had. His old handler, Feklisov, picked up the medal for him, since Fuchs was already dead.

Acknowledgments

Thank you to my agent, Carrie Pestritto, for always looking ahead and for finding Sky Pony, the perfect publisher for this series; to Alison Weiss for stepping in so valiantly and lovingly; to Emma Dubin for asking the hard questions; to Bethany Straker for capturing my voice in pictures; to Dr. Dian Murray for rising magnificently to my questions about Madame Cheng by sending me her life's work with no second thought; to Dr. David Perry for sharing with me his knowledge and chapters on relic theft; to Dr. Thomas Dale for posting his work on the Venetians for all; to Joe Medeiros for spending a morning discussing Vincenzo Peruggia (two Gs!); any mistakes are my own.

To my ever-supportive family and friends—I love you all. From planning book launches, supporting my books in your schools, making jokes, watching my kids during crunch time, and helping me locate hard-to-find articles, you've been a great village.

My husband doesn't get enough credit for all the help he gives me. Having a newborn isn't easy under the best circumstances. Having a book due while in labor is supremely bad timing. Thank you, Tim, for helping me read through *Fantastic Fugitives* while at the hospital, and all the little things you did at home to empower me to finish this book.

If You're Doing a Report . . .

The information in this book was intentionally presented in a way that makes it fun and easy to read, but if you'd like to learn more about any of the figures or if you need detailed information for a school project or report, you're in luck! Just visit www.briannadumont.com to download my citations and find tons of extra facts that didn't make it in the book!

Notes on Sources

Chapter One

The Venetians chapter was where I relied on the generosity of scholars the most. I personally contacted two for their takes on Venetian looting, since they dedicate their lives to primary sources. Thank you, again, Dr. David Perry and Dr. Thomas Dale for sharing your knowledge!

Chapter Two

Many myths surround Cortez and Pizarro, like that Cortez was the first conquistador or that conquistadors were all military trained and won despite being greatly outnumbered. Historian Matthew Restall puts those rumors to rest with his book *Seven Myths of the Spanish Conquest*. (Most conquistadors were ragtag dreamers with no experience, and they certainly weren't out-numbered, since they rounded up thousands of natives to fight with them.) The primary-source accounts I used are mostly from Spanish eyewitnesses, which means they all have a bias. The one Inca account was written decades after it happened. This all means that historians, myself included, have to play a bit of a guessing game, putting together leftover pieces of a puzzle with their own interpretations to make one big picture.

Chapter Three

England loves its warrior queen and so do biographers. I used modern historians' books for up-to-date analyses of her defeat of the Armada, and looked at one of Sir Francis Drake, that scoundrel.

Chapter Four

You don't get to be Great without a little blood on your hands in history. Just ask Catherine the Great, an unexpected thief. I looked to Robert K. Massie and Catherine's own diaries, which ended up being a lot of propaganda for the queen. Who better to tell your story than yourself? Just remember that it's only one side of the story, if you decide to read her diary yourself.

Chapter Five

When you're as fascinating as Napoleon, people are bound to write on a forest's worth of paper about you. The soldiers sent to guard over his deathbed on Elba couldn't help but spend most of their time writing in their diaries about the old general, hoping for blockbuster book deals once he kicked the bucket. Napoleon is also fascinatingly polarizing. He's a love-him-or-hate-him kind of guy. I choose to look at a variety of biographies in order to see both sides, and spent most of my time reading about Denon and the creation of the Louvre, since it's through his minister that Napoleon implemented the grand changes I'm concerned with in this chapter.

Chapter Six

How much do you wish Madame Cheng had left an autobiography? The things she might say . . . Instead, Dr. Dian Murray graciously shared with me her books and articles, written over years of research. The Royal Naval

Museum was also helpful, as well as books on both Western- and Eastern-style pirates. For more information on the effect of Confucianism on gender roles in nineteenth-century China, see *Women and Confucian Cultures in Premodern China, Korea, and Japan*, edited by Dorothy Ko.

Chapter Seven

Finding Fortune's story was a fortune indeed. (Sorry, I couldn't resist.) He's what started this whole journey of deciding to write a book about changing history. Eventually, that story morphed into this series. I loved reading his own words, which should be taken with a grain of salt and a cup of tea, and Sarah Rose's book *For All the Tea in China*. To be able to peek into forbidden China, and go where there be dragons, was no work at all.

Chapter Eight

Robert Smalls should have fame outside of Beaufort. He accomplished amazing feats of courage, and I'm not just talking about thieving. I put as much primary-source research into this chapter as I could, but also read Dr. Uya and Dr. Miller's takes on the thief-turned-statesman.

Chapter Nine

Boss Tweed wasn't one of the good guys; there's no way around that. He's a man of his times who took what advantages he could. I loved the idea that Kenneth D. Ackerman puts forth that the Boss *is* New York. He's big, fast, and full of that New York swagger. Like the city he helped create, he's larger than life.

Chapter Ten

Edison is a luminary of the Western world, and not just because he "invented" the lightbulb (which happened about the same way he "invented" most things in his life—by relying on others and then taking the credit). If you download the extra citation material, you might notice there are many more footnotes in Edison's chapter than in the others; I wanted to be sure readers would realize the extent to which scholars have debated Thomas Edison. I looked at both his critics and his fans (including the official editor of Edison's papers, Dr. Paul Israel) in order to get a rounded picture. I also read the work of early film historians to learn about the history of Hollywood.

Chapter Eleven

By utilizing secondary sources, I was able to come up with a lot of insight into what happened that fateful day in August when Peruggia stole the *Mona Lisa*. Of course, Vincenzo didn't leave any memoirs, and many of the sources don't agree on the specifics, which is reflected in the chapter. For example, two other versions include the plumber helping him escape, and a story about two other men helping Vincenzo on behalf of criminal mastermind Eduardo de Valiferno who intended to sell forgeries as the real deal, however there is no evidence such a man existed. I am grateful to the scholars and independent researchers who spent decades researching this long-forgotten thief. I find him just as enthralling as you do.

Chapter Twelve

Fuchs is another one of those liar/thief or patriot type of guys—it all depends on perspective. Of course, Fuchs wasn't the only atomic spy during this time. But he had no idea about the others in the United States, such as George Kovall in nuclear labs in Tennessee and Ohio or even those in Fuchs's own research facility like Ted Hall! Some documents about the development of the nuclear bombs are still classified today, meaning we still don't know their top-secret names. But historians like Allen Hornblum note that Fuchs has been called "by far the most important" atomic spy by multiple sources. It's also still debated as to who ratted first. Hornblum believes it was just good old-fashioned detective work. Feklisov says Gold ratted first, and others think it was Fuchs.

Sources

Chapter One

Classen, Albrecht, ed. *Urban Space in the Middle Ages and the Early Modern Age*. Berlin: W. de Gruyter, 2009.

Crowley, Roger. *City of Fortune: How Venice Ruled the Seas*. New York: Random House, 2011.

Dale, Thomas E. A. "Cultural Hybridity in Medieval Venice: Re-inventing the East at San Marco after the Fourth Crusade." In *San Marco, Byzantium and the Myths of Venice*, ed. Henry Maguire and Robert S. Nelson. Washington, D. C.: Dumbarton Oaks, 2010, 151–91.

Freeman, Charles. *The Horses of St. Mark: A Story of Triumph in Byzantium, Paris, and Venice*. New York: Overlook Press, 2004.

Hunt, Patrick. "Late Roman Silk: Smuggling and Espionage in the 6th Century CE." Philolog, Stanford University (blog).

Madden, Thomas. *Enrico Dandolo and the Rise of Venice*. Baltimore, MD: John Hopkins University Press, 2003.

Madden, Thomas. *Venice: A New History.* New York: Viking, 2012.

Miles, Margaret M. *Art as Plunder: The Ancient Origins of Debate about Cultural Property*. Cambridge: Cambridge University Press, 2008.

Nelson, Robert S. "High Justice: Venice, San Marco, and the Spoils of 1204." In *Byzantine Art in the Aftermath of the Fourth Crusade*, ed. Panayotis L. Vocotopoulos. Athens, Greece: Academy of Athens, 143–51. Found at: http://www.academia.edu/3624676/High_Justice_Venice_San_Marco_and_the_Spoils_of_1204. Accessed June 26, 2015.

Perry, David M. *Sacred Plunder: Venice and the Aftermath of the Fourth Crusade*. University Park: Penn State University Press, 2015.

Phillips, Jonathan. *The Fourth Crusade and the Sack of Constantinople*. New York: Viking, 2004.

Chapter Two

Bernstein, Peter L. *The Power of Gold: The History of an Obsession*. New York: John Wiley & Sons, 2000.

Burns, Kathryn. *Into the Archive: Writing and Power in Colonial Peru*. Durham, NC: Duke University Press, 2010.

Cocker, Mark. *Rivers of Blood, Rivers of Gold: Europe's Conquest of Indigenous Peoples*. New York: Grove Press, 1998.

Cowen, Richard. "New World Silver." Exploiting the Earth. 1999. Accessed August 23, 2016. http://mygeologypage.ucdavis.edu/cowen/~gel115/115ch8.html.

Gabai, Rafael Varón. *Francisco Pizarro and His Brothers: The Illusion of Power in Sixteenth-Century Peru*. Translated by Javier Flores Espinoza. Norman: University of Oklahoma Press, 1997.

Hemming, John. *The Conquest of the Incas*. New York: Harcourt, 1970.

Jones, Julie. "Gold of the Indies." Heilbrunn Timeline of Art History. New York: Metropolitan Museum of Art (October 2002). http://www.metmuseum.org/toah/hd/ingd/hd_ingd.htm

MacQuarrie, Kim. *The Last Days of the Incas*. New York: Simon & Schuster, 2007.

Nelson, Lynn Harry. "The Discovery of the New World and the End of the Old." Lectures in Medieval History. Accessed August 23, 2016. http://www.vlib.us/medieval/lectures/discovery.html.

Owen, James. "Lost Inca Gold: Ransom, Riches, and Riddles." National Geographic. Accessed August 23, 2016. http://science.nationalgeographic.com/science/archaeology/lost-inca-gold/.

Vassberg, David E. "Concerning Pigs, the Pizarros, and the Agro-Pastoral Background of the Conquerors of Peru." *Latin American Research Review* 13, no. 3 (1978): 47–61.

Chapter Three

BBC. "Beginner's Guide to Bowls." BBC Sport. Accessed July 16, 2015. http://news.bbc.co.uk/sport2/hi/other_sports/bowls/4747148.stm.

Cowen, Richard. "New World Silver." Exploiting the Earth. 1999. Accessed August 23, 2016. http://mygeologypage.ucdavis.edu/cowen/~gel115/115ch8.html.

"Elizabeth's Tilbury Speech." Timelines: Sources from History at the British Library. Accessed January 31, 2018. http://www.bl.uk/learning/timeline/item102878.html.

Hutchinson, Robert. *The Spanish Armada*. New York: Thomas Dunne, 2013.

Kelsey, Harry. *Sir Francis Drake: The Queen's Pirate*. New Haven, CT: Yale University Press, 1998.

McDermott, James. *England and the Spanish Armada: The Necessary Quarrel*. New Haven, CT: Yale University Press, 2005.

Patterson, Benton Rain. *With the Heart of a King*. New York: St. Martin's, 2007.

Trueman, C. N. "Philip and Religion." The History Learning Site. Accessed July 16, 2015. http://www.historylearningsite.co.uk/spain-under-phillip-ii/phillip-and-religion/.

Chapter Four

Catherine the Great. *The Memoirs of Catherine the Great*. Translated by Mark Cruse and Hilde Hoogenboom. New York: Modern Library, 2005.

de Madariaga, Isabel. *Catherine the Great: A Short History*. New Haven, CT: Yale University Press, 2002.

Dixon, Simon. *Catherine the Great*. New York: HarperCollins, 2009.

Leonard, Carol S. *Reform and Regicide: The Reign of Peter III of Russia*. Bloomington: Indiana University Press, 1993.

Lin, Diana. "Enlightened Monarchs of Europe." 2002. Accessed June 16, 2016. http://www.iun.edu/~hisdcl/h114_2002/enlightenedmonarchs.htm.

Longworth, Philip. "The Pretender Phenomenon in Eighteenth-Century Russia." Past and Present 66, no. 1 (1975): 61–83. https://academic.oup.com/past/article-abstract/66/1/61/1495715.

Massie, Robert K. *Catherine the Great: Portrait of a Woman*. New York: Random House, 2011.

Rounding, Virginia. *Catherine the Great: Love, Sex, and Power*. New York: St. Martin's Griffin, 2009.

Widener, Mike. "Monuments of Imperial Russian Law: The Nakaz in English." Yale Law School Library. 2012. Accessed June 16, 2016. http://library.law.yale.edu/news/monuments-imperial-russian-law-nakaz-english.

Chapter Five

"7.4 Million Visitors to the Louvre in 2016." Louvre. August 3, 2017. Accessed November 29, 2017. http://presse.louvre.fr/7-3-million-visitors-to-the-louvre-in-2016/.

Alexander, Edward P. *Museum Masters: Their Museums and Their Influence*. Walnut Creek, CA: AltaMira, 1995.

———. *Museums in Motion: An Introduction to the History and Functions of Museums*. Walnut Creek, CA: AltaMira, 1996.

Belting, Hans. *The Invisible Masterpiece*. Chicago: University of Chicago Press, 2001.

Denon, Vivant. *Travels in Upper and Lower Egypt: In Company with Several Divisions of the French Army, during the Campaigns of General Bonaparte in that Country*. Translated by Arthur Aikin. 1803. Reprint, Cambridge: Cambridge University Press, 2015.

Dunan, Marcel. "La taille de Napoleon." La Fondation Napoléon. Accessed August 31, 2016. http://www.napoleon.org/histoire-des-2-empires/articles/la-taille-de-napoleon/.

Forrest, Alan. *Napoleon: Life, Legacy, and Image: A Biography*. New York: St. Martin's Press, 2012.

Hicks, Peter. "What Did Napoleon do with the Horses on the Brandenburg Gate, Berlin?" La Fondation Napoléon. Accessed December 15, 2015. http://www.napoleon.org/en/reading_room/articles/files/napoleon_horses_brandenburg.asp.

Lindsay, Ivan. *The History of Loot and Stolen Art: From Antiquity until the Present Day*. London: Unicorn Press, 2014.

———. "The History of Collecting Old Masters." Lindsay Fine Art Blog. Entry posted February 1, 2010. Accessed September 13, 2016. http://www.old-masters.net/journal/the-history-of-collecting-old-masters/.

Meagher, Jennifer. "Orientalism in 19th Century Art." Heilbrunn Timeline of Art History. New York: The Metropolitan Museum of Art (October 2004). Accessed December 14, 2015. http://www.metmuseum.org/toah/hd/euor/hd_euor.htm.

McClellan, Andrew. *Inventing the Louvre: Art, Politics, and the Origins of the Modern Museum in Eighteenth-Century Paris*. Berkeley: University of California Press, 1994.

Miles, Margaret M. *Art as Plunder: The Ancient Origins of Debate about Cultural Property*. Cambridge: Cambridge University Press, 2008.

Oliver, Bette W. *From Royal to National: The Louvre Museum and the Bibliothèque Nationale*. New York: Lexington Books, 2007.

Roberts, Andrew. *Napoleon: A Life*. New York: Viking, 2014.

Chapter Six

Antony, Robert J. *Like Froth Floating on the Sea: The World of Pirates and Seafarers in Late Imperial South China*. Berkeley: University of California Press, 2003.

Cordingly, David. *Under the Black Flag: The Romance and Reality of Life among the Pirates*. New York: Random House, 2006.

Ellms, Charles. *The Pirates Own Book*. New York: Dover Publications, 1837. Found at: http://www.readcentral.com/book/Charles-Ellms/Read-The-Pirates-Own-Book-Online.

Ko, Dorothy, and JaHyun Kim Haboush, eds. *Women and Confucian Cultures in Premodern China, Korea, and Japan*. Berkeley: University of California Press, 2003.

Murray, Dian. "One Woman's Rise to Power: Cheng I's Wife and the Pirates." *Historical Reflections / Réflexions Historiques* 8, no. 3 (1981): 147–61. http://www.jstor.org/stable/41298765.

———. *Pirates of the South China Coast, 1790–1810*, Stanford, CA: Stanford University Press, 1987.

Pennell, C. R. *Bandits at Sea: A Pirates Reader*. New York: New York University Press, 2001.

Peterson, Willard J., ed. *The Cambridge History of China*, vol. 9. Cambridge: Cambridge University Press, 2002.

"Piracy: A Brief History of Piracy." Royal Naval Museum Library. Accessed October 8, 2014. http://www.royalnavalmuseum.org/info_sheets_piracy.htm.

Zelin, Madeleine. "Grandeur of the Qing Economy." Recording the Grandeur of the Qing. New York: Columbia University. Accessed May 30, 2015. http://www.learn.columbia.edu/nanxuntu/html/economy/.

Chapter Seven

"The Opium War and Foreign Encroachment." Asia for Educators. New York: Columbia University. Last modified 2009. Accessed July 30, 2015. http://afe.easia.columbia.edu/special/china_1750_opium.htm.

Fortune, Robert. *A Journey to the Tea Countries of China*. London: John Murray, 1852.

Kilpatrick, Ryan. "National Humiliation in China." Student thesis, University of Hong Kong, 2011. Accessed July 30, 2015. http://www.e-ir.info/2011/10/20/national-humiliation-in-china/.

Macfarlane, Alan. "The Empire of Tea." MPEG video, 35:35. University of Cambridge. February 5, 2013. Accessed July 30, 2015. http://upload.sms.cam.ac.uk/media/1402095.

Macfarlane, Iris and Alan. *The Empire of Tea: The Remarkable History of the Plant That Took Over the World*. New York: Overlook Press, 2004.

Mair, Victor H. *The True History of Tea*. London: Thames and Hudson, 2009.

Rose, Sarah. *For All the Tea in China: How England Stole the World's Most Famous Drink and Changed History*. New York: Viking, 2011.

Chapter Eight

Dawson, Victoria. "Copper Neck Tags Evoke the Experience of American Slaves Hired Out as Part-Time Laborers." *Smithsonian*. February 1, 2003. Accessed December 19, 2017. https://www.smithsonianmag.com/history/copper-neck-tags-evoke-experience-american-slaves-hired-out-part-time-laborers-76039831/.

Dray, Philip. *Capitol Men: The Epic Story of Reconstruction through the Lives of the First Black Congressmen*. Boston: Houghton Mifflin, 2008.

Freeman, Elsie, Wynell Burroughs Schamel, and Jean West. "The Fight for Equal Rights: A Recruiting Poster for Black Soldiers in the Civil War." *Social Education* 56, no. 2 (February 1992): 118–120. Accessed November 13, 2015. Found at: https://www.archives.gov/education/lessons/blacks-civil-war/.

Gonzalez, Julieta. "Group Calls for Repeal of Segregation-Era Laws Still on the Books." UANews. February 24, 2004. Accessed December 20, 2017. https://uanews.arizona.edu/story/group-calls-repeal-segregationera-laws-still-books/.

Harper's Weekly, "The Steamer 'Planter' and Her Captor." June 14, 1862.

"Jim Crow Laws – Separate Is Not Equal." Smithsonian National Museum of American History Behring Center. Accessed December 20, 2017. http://americanhistory.si.edu/brown/history/1-segregated/jim-crow.html.

Lineberry, Cate. *Be Free or Die: The Amazing Story of Robert Smalls' Escape from Slavery to Union Hero*. New York: St. Martin's, 2017.

Miller, Edward A., Jr. *Gullah Statesman: Robert Smalls from Slavery to Congress, 1839–1915*. Columbia: University of South Carolina Press, 1995.

Salvatore, Susan Cianci, ed. "Civil Rights: Racial Desegregation of Public Accommodations." PDF file. National Park Service. Accessed November 13, 2015. http://www.nps.gov/nhl/learn/themes/CivilRights_DesegPublicAccom.pdf.

United States House of Representatives. "Robert Smalls." History, Art, and Archives. Accessed November 13, 2015.
http://history.house.gov/People/Listing/S/SMALLS,-Robert-(S000502)/.

Uya, Okon. *From Slavery to Public Service: Robert Smalls, 1839–1915*. New York: Oxford University Press, 1971.

Chapter Nine

Ackerman, Kenneth D. *Boss Tweed: The Rise and Fall of the Corrupt Pol Who Conceived the Soul of Modern New York*. New York: Carroll & Graf Publishers, 2005.

Burrows, Edwin G., and Mike Wallace. *Gotham: A History of New York City to 1898*. New York: Oxford University Press, 1999.

Golway, Terry. *Machine Made: Tammany Hall and the Creation of Modern American Politics*. New York: Liveright, 2014.

Halloran, Fiona Deans. *Thomas Nast: The Father of Modern Political Cartoons*. Chapel Hill: University of North Carolina Press, 2012.

Kornfeld, Robert J., Jr. "Jerome Park Reservoir and the History of the Croton Waterworks." Lehman College. Accessed November 24, 2015. http://www.lehman.cuny.edu/lehman/preservationreport/history.html.

Mandelbaum, Seymour. *Boss Tweed's New York*. New York: John Wiley & Sons, 1965.

Mintz, S., and S. McNeil. "Boss Tweed." *Digital History*. Accessed November 24, 2015. http://www.digitalhistory.uh.edu/disp_textbook.cfm?smtID=2&psid=3052.

Tietjen, Lib. "If You Do the Crime, You've Got to Do the Time." Notes from the Tenement. Last modified May 2014. Accessed November 24, 2015. https://www.tenement.org/blog/if-you-do-the-crime-youve-got-to-do-the-time/.

Chapter Ten

Bowser, Eileen. *The Transformation of Cinema to 1907*. New York: Scribner, 1990.

———. *The Transformation of Cinema 1907–1915*. New York: Scribner, 1990.

Brown, Richard. "William Kennedy-Laurie Dickson." Who's Who of Victorian Cinema. Accessed May 5, 2016. http://www.victorian-cinema.net/dickson.

Decherney, Peter. *Hollywood's Copyright Wars: From Edison to the Internet*. New York: Columbia University Press, 2012.

"Edison and Tesla." *Ten Things You Don't Know About,* Season 3, Episode 4. History.com. A&E Networks. Paul Israel (Interview). 6 September, 2014. Accessed September 6, 2016. http://www.history.com/shows/10-things-you-dont-know-about/season-3/episode-4/edisons-spirit-phone/.

Edison Innovation Foundation. "Edison Patents." Thomas A. Edison. Last modified 2014. Accessed May 2, 2016. https://www.thomasedison.org/edison-patents /.

Franco, Armando. "The Motion Picture Patents Company vs. The Independent Outlaws." Lecture, May 2004. University of California, Berkeley. Accessed May 6, 2016. http://are.berkeley.edu/%7Esberto/EEP142Project.pdf.

"Guide to Motion Picture Catalogs." The Thomas A. Edison Papers. 2013. Accessed September 06, 2016. http://edison.rutgers.edu/mopix/mopix.htm.

Hart, Terry. "Was Hollywood Built on Piracy?" *Copyhype*. Last modified May 7, 2012. Accessed, May 7, 2016. http://www.copyhype.com/2012/05/was-hollywood-built-on-piracy/.

McDonald, Paul, Eric Hoyt, Emily Carman, and Philip Drake, eds. *Hollywood and the Law*. London: British Film Institute, 2015.

Musser, Charles. *Before the Nickelodeon*. Berkeley: University of California Press, 1991.

Olson-Raymer, Gayle. "The Entertainment and Theme Park Industries." Humboldt State University. Accessed May 7, 2016. http://users.humboldt.edu/ogayle/hist383/Entertainment.html.

Robinson, David. "Marie-Georges-Jean Méliès." Who's Who of Victorian Cinema. Accessed May 6, 2016. http://www.victorian-cinema.net/melies.

Sklar, Robert. *Movie-Made America: A Cultural History of American Movies*. New York: Vintage, 1994.

Stross, Randall. *The Wizard of Menlo Park: How Thomas Alva Edison Invented the Modern World*. New York: Crown, 2007.

The Thomas Edison Center at Menlo Park. Visitor Information. Accessed October 14, 2016. http://www.menloparkmuseum.org.

United States v. Motion Picture Patents Co et. al., 225 F. 800 (3d Cir. Oct. 1, 1915). Accessed May 7, 2016. https://archive.org/stream/gov.uscourts.f1.225/225.f1#page/n815/mode/2up.

Chapter Eleven

Belting, Hans. *The Invisible Masterpiece*. Chicago: University of Chicago Press, 2001.

Charney, Noah. *The Thefts of the Mona Lisa: On Stealing the World's Most Famous Painting*. Association for Research into Crimes against Art, 2011.

Esterow, Milton. *The Art Stealers*. New York: Macmillan, 1973.

Hales, Dianne. *Mona Lisa: A Life*. New York: Simon & Schuster, 2014.

Mona Lisa Is Missing. Directed by Joe Medeiros. Virgil Films, 2012.

Public Broadcasting Service. "Leonardo's Masterful Technique." Treasures of the World. Accessed October 1, 2015. http://www.pbs.org/treasuresoftheworld/a_nav/mona_nav/mnav_level_1/3technique_monafrm.html.

Scotti, R. A. *Vanished Smile: The Mysterious Theft of the Mona Lisa*. New York: Vintage, 2010.

Tandy, Joseph. "Frustrated Russian Throws Cup at Mona Lisa." *Reuters*. August 11, 2009. Accessed October 1, 2015. https://www.reuters.com/article/us-france-monalisa/frustrated-russian-throws-cup-at-mona-lisa-idUSTRE57A2JS20090811.

Chapter Twelve

Bernstein, Jeremy. "John Von Neumann and Klaus Fuchs: An Unlikely Collaboration." *Physics in Perspective* 12, no. 1 (March 2010): 36–50.

Caltech. "How Hot Is the Sun؟" Cool Cosmos. Accessed September 26, 2016. http://coolcosmos.ipac.caltech.edu/ask/7-How-hot-is-the-Sun-.

DNewsChannel. "Hydrogen Bomb vs. Atomic Bomb: What's The Difference؟" YouTube. January 10, 2016. Accessed September 23, 2016. https://www.youtube.com/watch؟v=bwAh3Z0shsE.

Feklisov, Alexander. *The Man Behind the Rosenbergs*. New York: Enigma Books, 2004.

"Hiroshima and Nagasaki Death Toll." Children of the Atom Bom. October 2007. Accessed November 30, 2017. http://www.aasc.ucla.edu/cab/200708230009.html.

Holloway, David. *Stalin and the Bomb*. New Haven, CT: Yale University Press, 1994.

Hornblum, Allen. *The Invisible Harry Gold: The Man Who Gave the Soviets the Atom Bomb*. New Haven, CT: Yale University Press, 2010.

"Language of Espionage." International Spy Museum. Accessed September 27, 2016. https://www.spymuseum.org/education-programs/news-books-briefings/language-of-espionage/.

Linder, Doug. "Trial of the Rosenbergs: An Account." Famous Trials. Last modified 2011. Accessed September 27, 2016. http://law2.umkc.edu/faculty/projects/ftrials/rosenb/ROS_ACCT.HTM.

Rhodes, Richard. *Dark Sun: The Making of the Hydrogen Bomb*. New York: Simon & Schuster, 1995.

"The Potsdam Conference, 1945." Office of the Historian, United States Department of State. Accessed September 28, 2016. https://history.state.gov/milestones/1937-1945/potsdam-conf.

Weinstein, Allen, and Alexander Vassiliev. *The Haunted Wood: Soviet Espionage in America—The Stalin Era*. New York: Modern Library, 1999.

Image Credits

Chapter One

Venice: A Regatta on the Grand Canal by Canaletto in 1735, courtesy of Wikipedia Commons Public Domain / Source: National Gallery in London via Oursana in 2016.

Translation of St. Mark over right portal in St. Mark's Basilica, courtesy of Louis H. Hamel, Jr.

Kingdom of Italy map, courtesy of Wikipedia Commons Public Domain / Source: *Cambridge Modern History Atlas* 1912 via DIREKTOR in 2012.

The Crusaders Conquering the City of Zara in 1202 by Andrea Vicentino, courtesy of Wikipedia Commons Public Domain / Source: Sala del Maggior Consiglio via Tzowu in 2015.

Seawalls in Constantinople, Turkey, courtesy of Wikimedia Commons / CC BY-SA 3.0 by author Ollios in 2013.

The Tetrarchs in Venice, Italy, courtesy of Wikimedia Commons / CC BY-SA 3.0 by author Nino Barbieri in 2007.

Horses of Basilica San Marco in Venice, Italy, courtesy of Wikimedia Commons / CC BY-SA 3.0 by author Morn in 2011.

Chapter Two

Portrait of Francisco Pizarro by Amable-Paul Coutan in 1835, courtesy of Wikipedia Commons Public Domain / Source: Palace of Versailles Museum via ORGPE in 2016

Pizarro Meets Atahualpa, 1532 by Waman Poma de Ayala in 17th century, courtesy of Wikipedia Commons Public Domain / Source: Royal Library of Denmark via Ferbr1 in 2010.

Ransom Room of Atahualpa in Cajamarca, courtesy of Wikimedia Commons / CC BY-SA 3.0 by author Antonio Velasco in 2005.

Blank Map Caribbean Sea, courtesy of Wikipedia Commons Public Domain / Source: Lencer in 2007.

Incan Kipu, talking knots, courtesy of iStock / Source: andyKRAKOVSKI in 2016.

Chapter Three

The Ermine Portrait of Elizabeth I of England by William Segar in 1585, courtesy of Wikipedia Commons Public Domain / Source: Hatfield House via Kaho Mitsuki in 2017.

Philip II in Armor by Titian in 1551, courtesy of Wikipedia Commons Public Domain / Source: Prado Museum via Crisco 1492 in 2014.

A Naval Encounter between Dutch and Spanish Warships by Cornelis Verbeeck in 1620 courtesy of Wikipedia Commons Public Domain / Source: National Gallery of Art via Christoph Braun in 2014 .

Drake Knighted by Joseph Boehm in 1883, courtesy of Wikipedia Commons Public Domain / Source: Statue base in Tavistock, Devon, via Lobsterthermidor in 2011.

Portrait of Elizabeth I of England, the Armada Portrait by Anonymous circa 1588, courtesy of Wikipedia Commons Public Domain / Source: Woburn Abbey via Buchraeumer in 2010.

Routes of the Spanish Armada, courtesy of Wikipedia Commons Public Domain / Source: History Department of the United States Military Academy at West Point via Kooma in 2006.

Chapter Four

Portrait of Grand Duke Peter Fedorovich (Later Emperor Peter III) by Georg Cristoph Grooth in 1743, courtesy of Wikipedia Commons Public Domain / Source: Tretyakov Gallery via Shakko in 2011.

Map of Europe, 1815, courtesy of Wikipedia Commons Public Domain / Source: The International Commission and Association on Nobility via Ras67 in 2015.

Catherine II of Russia accompanied by the army at St Petersburg, courtesy of iStock / Source: *Cassell's Illustrated History of England (1820-1861)* via Cannasue in 2018.

Vaccination against Small Pox by Isaac Cruikshank in 1808, courtesy of Wellcome Collection

Chapter Five

United States Expansion by the United States Government in 2000s, courtesy of Wikipedia Commons Public Domain / Source: *National Atlas of the United States* via Peteforsyth in 2013.

Robespierre executant le bourreau by H. Fleischmann in 1908, courtesy of Wikipedia Commons Public Domain / Source: *La Guillotine en 1793* via Emmanuel.boutet in 2011.

Apollo Belvedere by Anonymous Roman artist, courtesy of Wikipedia Commons Public Domain / Source: Vatican Museums via Livioandronico2013 in 2014.

Battle of the Pyramids by Louis-François Lejeune in 1808, courtesy of Wikipedia Commons Public Domain / Source: Palace of Versailles Museum via Bogomolov.PL in 2012.

Vivant Denon by Robert Lefèvre in 1808, courtesy of Wikipedia Commons Public Domain / Source: Palace of Versailles Museum via Mu in 2006.

Wedding Procession of Napoleon and Marie-Louise by Benjamin Zix in 1810, courtesy of Wikipedia Commons Public Domain / Source: Louvre Museum via Raymond Ellis in 2013.

Chapter Six

Guangzhou Chinese Boats by Lai Afong circa 1880, courtesy of Wikipedia Commons Public Domain / Source: Scewing in 2015.

Southeast Asia (Reference Map), courtesy of the University of Texas Libraries / Source: U.S. Central Intelligence Agency in 2013.

Piracy of the South China Sea from Qing scroll in Hong Kong Maritime Museum, courtesy of Wikimedia Commons / CC BY-SA 3.0 by author Triotriotrio in 2012.

Jianqing Emperor by Anonymous Qing Dynasty Court Painter in 17th Century, courtesy of Wikipedia Commons Public Domain / Source: Palace Museum in Beijing via Qingprof in 2011.

Chapter Seven

Papaver somniferum, courtesy of Wikipedia Commons Public Domain / Source: Prof. Dr. Otto Wilhelm Thomé *Flora von Deutschland, Österreich und der Schweiz 1885* via Topjabot in 2004.

Camellia sinensis, courtesy of Wikipedia Commons Public Domain / Source: Franz Eugen Köhler's Medizinal-Pflanzen in 1897 via Sergey Liverko in 2010.

Nemesis Destroying Chinese Junks by Edward Duncan in 1843, courtesy of Wikipedia Commons Public Domain / Source: Royal Collection Trust via Spellcast in 2016

Tea Plantation in Hangzhou, courtesy of Wikimedia Commons / CC BY-SA 1.0 by author Shizhao in 2005.

Terrarium for tropical rainforest pets, courtesy of iStock / Source: kikkerdick in 2013.

Chapter Eight

Slave Badge from 1825, Courtesy of The Charleston Museum, Charleston, South Carolina.

The Gun-Boat *Planter*, courtesy of Wikipedia Commons Public Domain / Source: Harper's Weekly June 14th, 1862 via Mojoworker in 2014.

Field Artillery, used in the War of 1864, 24 pounder shell gun of army 1834, courtesy of Wikimedia Commons / Source: author Alf van Beem in 2013.

4th United States Colored Infantry in 1864, courtesy of Wikipedia Commons Public Domain / Source: Library of Congress via Kimse in 2008.

Robert Smalls photographed by Matthew Brady in 1870s, courtesy of Wikipedia Commons Public Domain / Source: Library of Congress via Adam Cuerden in 2016.

Colored Waiting Room Sign by Esther Bubley in 1943, courtesy of Wikipedia Commons Public Domain / Source: Library of Congress via Ras67 in 2015.

Chapter Nine

Boss Tweed "The Brains" by Thomas Nast in 1871, courtesy of Wikipedia Commons Public Domain / Source: Harper & Brothers via WFinch in 2016.

Americus Engine Co. No. 6 Soiree Ticket by Louis Oram in 1887, courtesy of Wikipedia Commons Public Domain / Source: NYPL Digital Gallery via Beyond My Ken in 2010.

Boss Tweed "The Ballots" by Thomas Nast in 1871, courtesy of Wikipedia Commons Public Domain / Source: Harper & Brothers via Storkk in 2007.

Boss Tweed in Jail by Thomas Nast in 1872, courtesy of Wikipedia Commons Public Domain / Source: Harper & Brothers via Howcheng in 2012.

Chapter Ten

Kinetophone in 1895, courtesy of Wikipedia Commons Public Domain / Source: Victorian Cinema via Stef48 in 2007.

Thomas Edison and the perfected phonograph in 1888, courtesy of Wikipedia Commons Public Domain / Source: NPS Thomas Edison National Historic Park via Marrante in 2012.

Melies color Voyage dans la lune by Georges Méliès in 1902, courtesy of Wikipedia Commons Public Domain / Source: screenshot via Lemuellio in 2013.

Screenshot from *The Great Train Robberty* by Edwin S. Porter in 1903, courtesy of Wikipedia Commons Public Domain / Source: screenshot via Sailko.

Edison Motion Picture Studio in 1914, courtesy of Wikipedia Commons Public Domain / Source: *A Pictorial History of the Movies* via We hope in 2015.

Chapter Eleven

Mona Lisa by Leonardo da Vinci in 1506, courtesy of Wikipedia Commons Public Domain / Source: Louvre Museum via Cybershot800i in 2011.

Alphonse Bertillon in 1912, courtesy of Wikimedia Commons / CC BY-SA 1.0 by author Jebulon in 2014.

Stolen Mona Lisa in 1911, courtesy of Wikipedia Commons Public Domain / Source: "The Two Mona Lisas" in Century Magazine via Shakko in 2018.

Mona Lisa Uffizi in 1913, courtesy of Wikipedia Commons Public Domain / Source: *The Telegraph* via Fma12 in 2014.

Crowd Looking at the Mona Lisa at the Louvre, courtesy of Wikimedia Commons / CC BY-SA 4.0 by author Victor Grigas in 2014.

Chapter Twelve

Klaus Fuchs Police Photograph in 1940, courtesy of Wikipedia Commons Public Domain / Source: The National Archives UK via Bomazi in 2011.

Trinity Test Shot Color by photographer Jack W. Aeby in 1945, courtesy of Wikipedia Commons Public Domain / Source: *Life* Photo Archive via Hawkeye7 in 2014.

Venona Project in 1940s, courtesy of Wikipedia Commons Public Domain / Source: United States Department of Energy via Magnus Manske in 2010.

Julius and Ethel Rosenberg by photographer Roger Higgins in 1951, courtesy of Wikipedia Commons Public Domain / Source: Library of Congress via Davepape in 2006.

Potsdam Conference group portrait, July 1945, courtesy of Wikipedia Commons Public Domain / Source: Presidential Collection of Harry S. Truman via Scewing in 2010.

Index